ISBN: 978-0-578-92751-0

Printed by Power Of Purpose Publishing
Www.PopPublishing.com
Atlanta, Ga. 30326

Saturday Morning Rain

To My Mother Betty
Whose life inspired me to be better, dig deeper,
and write… I miss you, Rest in Heaven.

To My Husband Cedric, our three children;
Mckinis, Cedric Jr., and India
Thank you for your love, support, and patience as I walked
through this journey of expression, I love you all…

PREFACE

Nadine is a wife, mother and minister who deals with the heartache of a broken marriage- troubled relationship with her daughter and family secrets from her father that forces her to make tough decisions all while she battles breast cancer.

Her father, a prominent pastor in the community, is dying from lung cancer. He passes the church to his son in law Jeffrey, who takes the church in a whole new direction from the legacy it was built on. There is scandal and infidelity, death and healing all rolled up in this story. Nadine falls in love with her nurse Todd, after her husband hires him to take care of her after her mastectomy.

CHAPTER ONE

A Rainy Day Indeed

It's 6:00 a.m and I'm awake, it's too early to get up for church but I'm up. I've been up for a while, couldn't go back to sleep because this man is snoring. I hear the rain coming down, I love the sound of it. It is so peaceful. The wind is blowing pretty hard, I guess I better get up and close the bay window. In Indiana, you can sleep with the windows open at night, enjoy the cool breeze that comes through in the summertime, what my mama calls "the cool night air." The rain drops are coming through the window screen so I better close the window fast.

As I move towards the seat of the bay window, I sit down for a minute. I think back on the good old days when we were kids. Me and my older brother RJ used to love to play in the rain; especially on a Saturday morning. We didn't have to worry about going to school, and mama would let us dance and jump in puddles of water until the rain would leave at the end of our driveway. We had yellow raincoats and yellow rain boots to match. Mama would say, "You can play in the rain only for a while, but you better come inside before your daddy gets home."Life was so sweet then, I loved my family so much, especially my mama, she was the best in the world in my eyes. Dad and I were close too, he tried to pretend he was tough on the outside but in reality, he was a cuddly teddy bear. I chuckle under my breath as I think about the good old days when life was so simple.

"Are you just gonna sit there and let the rain come, in or you gonna close the darn window?" He asked. I didn't even know the mean giant was up! He ruined my day dreaming moment with his loud and stern voice. He never woke up pleasant, always finding something to grumble about. His name is Jeffrey, my husband, but I call him the mean giant, you get it, instead of the Jolly green giant, he's the mean giant, standing at 6'3. There's nothing jolly about this man. I don't know what happened, he used to be so sweet but since he became partner in his law firm 5 years ago, he got mean and ornery. I guess it's the pressure of work? I don't know, I don't really care anymore, let me close this window and go make some coffee, I can see it's gonna be one of those days.

My name is Nadine Broadnax, I'm a wife, a nurse and the mother of a beautiful set of twins, Brittany and Brandon. My kids are grown so it's just me and Jeff in the house, oh and my miniature toy terrier "Rollo, he's a joy. I find myself spending more time with Rollo than anyone else these days. Maybe I'm still going through empty nest syndrome? But the twins have been out of the house for about 3 years. Brandon is a radio engineer for some hip hop station in Chicago. He graduated from the University of Chicago with a degree in Mass Communications. Brittany, my daughter, graduated with her degree in Criminal Justice from Southern University in Louisiana, she lives in Houston now because she just graduated from Thurgood Marshall school of law. She's studying to take her bar exam and seems to be super busy because every time I call her, she doesn't have time to talk. She always says, "Mom, I can't talk now, you know I'm studying for the bar, I'll call you back." She never does. She's just like her father, very driven but very stubborn. Now, Brandon, he's a mama's boy, he calls me at least once a week, sometimes more, always wanting to know what I cooked for dinner as if he's going to come home and get a plate. He surprised me a few times by coming home for the weekend but since he got this new girlfriend, Gina, he hasn't been home in a few months, but he still calls his mama, I enjoy that.

Now that the coffee is brewing, I'm pretty sure Jeff wants eggs and toast before service. He always says it's good to eat breakfast before service so that people won't hear your stomach growling. I say it's good to eat breakfast and add a mint so you won't have what I call, "church brath". Church breath is extremely bad breath that you can smell from all sides. It don't make no sense that I can smell your breath and you're sitting behind me. I keep mints on hand and pass them out as a friendly gesture. I think most people have caught on to my hints though, some seem offended.

I walk upstairs to hand Jeff his plate, 2 eggs, sunny side up, 1 piece of toast, sliced with peach preserves. That's what he likes on Sundays, don't ask me why, he just does. I walk into the room and he's already dressed, looking in the mirror, adjusting his tie and I lay the plate on the table. "I'm not eating this morning", he said. I've got to get to the church early, your dad said he wanted to talk to me before service." Negro, why you didn't tell me? Is what I thought in my head but I would never say to him, at least not right before church. Well, there's coffee downstairs if you want a cup before you leave, I told him. He nodded, tightened his belt, grabbed his jacket, and walked out the door. "See you at church, love ya, bye", he said. Love you too, I told him as I looked out the window. The rain eased up by now. I grabbed my cup of coffee and tried to revisit the thoughts I had in my head upstairs, but it was too late. I had to get ready for church. I wonder what daddy has to talk to Jeff about today. Let me hurry so I can find out, it must be important.

CHAPTER TWO

The Big Announcement

"Good morning Sister Nadine", said the church greeter at the door. Good morning, I said as I walked quickly past the crowd in the vestibule. I didn't feel like socializing, I was trying to get to daddy's office so I can see what this meeting with Jeff was about. My daddy, Pastor Robert Lee Payne, was the pastor and founder of our church, Grace Christian Center. My mother, Elect Lady Diane Payne helped him build this church. They both put in a lot of sweat and tears to make this church what it is today. It's no mega church but with a membership of over 1500 on the roster, it still takes a lot of work to make things run smoothly around here. That's where I come in, daddy made me the Administrative Director a few years ago, only after mama said she was tired of doing it and she wanted to focus more on community charities. I only do it part time though and since mama still likes to take control of things, I thought it best I don't spend too much time at Grace.

Truth is, mama wants to be a socialite, she enjoyed hanging with her high society friends, sipping tea and gossiping about people. She and the other "first ladies" from our sister churches were a hot mess. Sweet as they could be but you bet not tell them your business, you might as well put it on the 5 o'clock news. Mama still had an office, she still wanted to feel important at church you know. As I zoom past her office, I hear her calling my name, "Naddie", is what she called me. Ma'am, I said. Come here for a minute. Oh Lord, what does she want? I'm trying to get to daddy's office to be nosey. I peek my head through her door, Good morning mama, what's up? What's up? She said, is that any way to greet your mama on this Sunday morning? I just stand there for a second, I don't know what else to say? I wanted to let you know that dad and I want you guys to come over for dinner this evening.

Okay, I said but I'm wondering why she didn't call me last night to tell me, I've already got steaks thawing out for dinner today. Does this have anything to do with daddy talking to Jeff this morning? I asked. What you mean, why are you being so nosey? She paused for a second then said yes, we want to talk to you and RJ. Me and RJ! I said with a loud voice. If RJ is coming then I know it's important! My older brother RJ rarely comes around anymore, he has some kind of complex because he thinks we don't like his wife because she's white. I don't like her because she's a gold-digging hussy! Nothing to do with her skin color.

My brother RJ is a restaurateur, he's a professional Chef and has 1 restaurant and 1 bakery here in Cedar City. He makes good money. He used to be married to Gloria, his high school sweetheart, she was black, well actually she was mixed with black and Puerto Rican. I really liked her but she couldn't have any kids. RJ divorced her for Shannon, who hurried up and popped out 3 kids to secure her stake in the financials if you know what I mean. I don't even think she loves RJ, she treats him like trash. Anyway, like I said, if RJ is coming to the meeting then I know something is up. So, I walked towards mama to give her a hug and tell her that we'll be there. Of course, you will darling, she said as she kissed me on my cheek. "Mama, you smell so good as always," I said. I loved the smell of mama, it wasn't so much of her perfume, it smells like peace. That's the only way I could describe it, it was her own personal scent. I remember smelling this same scent as a child, it was comforting.

So, I proceed on my mission to find out if daddy and Jeff are still talking. I know mama said they want to talk to us after service but I wanna know now! How do they expect me to sit through service wondering about this? I'm walking fast as ever, it seems as though dad's office is a mile away, I hit the corner turning left, and run right into Jeff. Oh- hey, I said, you coming from daddy's office? Yeah, where are you going? He asked, Well, I was going to talk to dad to see how he's doing. Well, he's praying right now, don't disturb him, come on. He grabs my arm and turns me around to walk down the hall with him. I'm livid! How dare you tell me not to go talk to my own daddy but you get up early to come and talk to him, that's MY daddy! But I never said a word, I learned to pick and choose my battles with Jeff, and arguing with him before service would just vex my spirit. Okay then, well I better get to the prayer room, I told Jeff. We parted ways and I headed down the hall. Okay, Naddie, get yourself together, I told myself. After all, I'm the lead intercessor, I had to get ready to do intercession with my team. I can't go before the Lord on behalf of the congregation mad at Jeff. "Father please forgive me and guard my heart against negative thoughts in Jesus' name. I said that quick prayer and opened the doors to the prayer room. Good morning everyone, I said to my prayer team, let's get ready to pray….

Service went on, daddy preached a good sermon, "When your brook dries up" coming from the scripture 1 Kings 17:7. I really enjoyed it but the service isn't over yet, he hasn't done the benediction. Dad stands at the podium, hands on each side as if he needed the podium to stand steady. Well, Grace family, he says as he prepares to make some sort of announcement. I wanted you all to know that next Sunday, my wife and family will be making an important announcement. I ask for your prayers and ask that you all be here next Sunday to hear this announcement. He stands in silence for a few seconds then closes with the benediction. I look around, I see the people in the congregation looking perplexed. People started whispering, wondering what is going to happen. I grab my purse and bible and head to my office, I don't want nobody asking me any questions because I don't even know what's going on. I get stopped a few times by members saying hello, some trying to look me in my eyes to see if I had been crying, people all around trying to figure things out, I'm just ready to go.

Oh Lord! I cry out loud in my head, here comes aunt Ruby! Nadine! Nadine, she calls, what's wrong with your daddy? Hey aunt Ruby, I said, as I reluctantly hugged her. Chile, what is your daddy talking about, she yelled. And why didn't he call me, what is going on? Aunt Ruby was my dad's only sister, I call her Nosey Rosey because she's always in somebody's business. I don't even know myself aunt Ruby, I told her as I had to squeeze myself from her fat arms. She always did hug too long and smelled like moth balls too. Girl you know, you just don't want to tell me, what is this announcement about? Robert knows he needs to be telling me what's going on, he ain't right! She yelled. Aunt Ruby, calm down, I'm sure daddy is going to tell all of us whatever it is he's talking about real soon, we just have to wait. Mmmm-Hmmm, she said, yall wrong, but that's okay, I'm gonna call him later. Bye aunt Ruby, I said as I waved my hand and walked away. That woman knows how to get on my nerves. All I could think about was this dinner meeting we were having at mama's house. I wouldn't dare tell Nosey Rosey about it and she bet not pop up over there either.

Once Jeff and I arrive home, I hurry to change clothes so I can get to my parent's house a little early. Jeff claims he has some emails to respond to as he stares hard into his laptop, pretending like he's so busy. I know that he's trying to avoid me asking him about his very private meeting with daddy. I want to ask him so badly but I know he won't tell me, he probably finds pleasure in knowing something that I don't know on my side of the family. He was close to daddy though- they always did get along great. Jeff's dad passed away when Jeff was in high school, I believe his mama drove that man into a heart attack. She was one evil lady. Jeff is an only child and she always reminds me of how I took her baby from her. I tell her, "Ms. Irene, you can always have him back whenever you want him", I always add a chuckle at the end so she'll think I'm joking, but sometimes I really mean it. Jeff and his mama aren't really that close, but he pays all her bills and stuff, whatever social security and veteran's benefits won't pay. Jeff's dad, Leroy was an Army veteran, he made a career out of being a soldier. Ms. Irene said Jeff has never been the same since Leroy passed, she thinks his dad's passing made Jeff mean, little does she know that Leroy told him he thinks his mama put a root on him when she found out he was cheating on her with a drill sergeant in Fort Dix, New Jersey. Jeff can't help but believe that the questionable root Irene put on his dad killed him, after all, he was the perfect bill of health. Being a sergeant in the Army kept him physically fit. I think the guilt of his adulterous affairs killed him, but I digress.

"Rollo, Rollo", I called out for my favorite dude, my little dog Rollo. Where is that boy? I peeked around the corner just to find him sitting on his dog bed with one eye open, acting like he didn't hear me calling his name. Come here, boy! I screamed, you gotta go potty? I asked him while I shook his leash. He got up real slow, stretching like I disturbed him from his nap. He walked slow, passed his freshly poured dog food, sniffed it, and kept walking. I let him outside to use the bathroom because I figured Jeff and I would be gone over mamas for a while. Mama wouldn't let me bring him over because he always chased mama's old ugly cat, Eartha Kit Kat, named after the actress Eartha Kitt. Yep, that's what she named that ugly orange-haired rascal. I hate that cat, she's fat and sneaky too, always staring at me like she doesn't want me to come to visit my own mama. I always sneak and lock her in the laundry room whenever I do visit. I tell her, "get in there, smell your own pee and doo-doo for a change!" That's where her litter box is. I know it's mean but I don't care, I hate that cat, I think she's full of evil spirits. Perhaps she should go live with Ms.Irene?

After I let Rollo back inside, I put the thawed steaks in the refrigerator and headed upstairs to get dressed. I'm expecting Jeff to be up and ready to roll like he was this morning, but as I walk through the bedroom door, I noticed he's fallen asleep on the bed, laptop in hand, and shoes on his feet. "I should just leave his butt here and go early," I say to myself but I'm pretty good at not treating people the same way they treat me. So I shake his foot, "babe, babe, as I shake a little harder. You changing clothes or are you ready to go? He wakes up, yawns and says he's gonna change clothes first. He puts his laptop down and walks into the closet and grabs his favorite pair of jeans. Well, he only has one pair and he wears them when he's feeling sure of himself like he's a mack daddy or something. I'm thinking this must be one heck of an announcement and Jeff is too proud to already know in advance if he's wearing those jeans. I take a peek at his laptop just to see if he really checked his emails. Come to find out, this fella been on Facebook. Really Jeff? So I slip on my favorite flats and wait for the mean giant to change clothes so we can head on out.

Jeff and I arrive at my parent's home. I can see RJ's SUV as we turn into the driveway. Oh! They made it here 1st, I said, with excitement in my voice. It doesn't matter who made it 1st Nadine, don't start, says Jeff. I side-eye him, reluctant to respond but I had to this time. Jeff, I wasn't meaning it like that, I'm just happy to see my brother and his kids, I said while rolling my eyes. What about Shannon? You should be happy to see her too, he said. "Shut up Jeff, let's not start with all that, of course, I'm happy to see Shannon too, I say with extreme sarcasm. I don't know why he's trying to pick a fight with me all of a sudden? Those comments were so unnecessary. I just zip my lip until we park the car and get out.

As I open the door, I see the cutest little brown-eyed 3-year old I've ever seen. "My little Lindsey, I screamed as I picked her up and gave her a million kisses. Lindsey was my youngest niece, she was so adorable and she loved me, her aunt Naddie. "Take this nook nook out your mouth," I tell her as I grab the pacifier from between her lips. I steal a kiss and hurry to put the nook nook back in. She's 3 years old for Pete's sake, she should not still be sucking on a pacifier but that's her lazy mama's fault, anything to make these kids shut up! She did Chad the same way, he's my 10-year-old nephew. Sucking on a pacifier til he was 5 is the reason why he's buck-toothed now. He's smart as a whip though, real good with math. I told RJ that Chad could do his books better than he can. Chad comes around the corner, Hey auntie! He said, while giving me a one-armed hug, not because he didn't like me but because he was always trying to pretend to be cool, boy, you still a nerd but I love ya!. I hug him back and kiss him on his cheek. He didn't know I saw him wipe it off once he turned the corner, I saw him in mama's huge mirror in the hallway. Jeff and I walk into the living room, everyone is sitting down looking confused, well, everyone except mom and dad.

Hey bro! I said to RJ, he stands up and gives me the biggest hug. We always loved and respected each other, even though we didn't care for one another's spouses. RJ hated Jeff but he tolerated him just like I did Shannon. RJ said Jeff was arrogant and always used big words for no reason, even though I know RJ was right, I still couldn't help but believe he was a little jealous of Jeff and dad's relationship. Hey Shannon, I said as I bent down to give her a hug too. She could've stood up but she's too lazy. I don't know why, she don't do nothing, talking about being a stay at home mom of 3 kids is hard. Chile, please 2 of your kids in school all day and she dopes up little Lindsey with cough syrup to keep her sleeping all day, but she don't think I know that. Girl, I'm a nurse, I know everything I say in my head sarcastically. Anyway, I look around and ask, where's Jessica? She's my 13-year-old niece, cute as pie but bad as hell. She gives my brother the blues, of course, she does, she acts just like her mama. "She's over there with them headphones stuck in her ears," RJ said. Yeah, she probably won't even know you're here, said Shannon.

First of all, she knows I'm here, she probably can't hear me but she can see me, I thought, secondly, the little heifer is so rude, she won't even come and greet me. So, I walked toward the recliner she was sitting in, tapped her on her leg, and said, "Hey pretty girl", I counted 5 seconds before she responded, Oh hey auntie, as if she didn't hear or see me at first. I said, "What are you listening to that got you so distracted?" "Beyonce," she said while rolling her eyes like I was disturbing her. I can hardly stand my own niece, she's too spoiled and has the smartest mouth in the world. I don't fool with her too much, I love her but like her mama, I don't like her. If I talked to Pastor the way she talked to my brother, all my teeth would be knocked out. I don't know how RJ put up with it?

So once we all sit down, Shannon tells Jessica to take the kids upstairs to the game room. "Why I gotta do it?" she screamed. Because she said so, RJ said with a stern tone. So she snatches up my little Lindsey, tells Chad to come on, and stomps upstairs.

Sooooo, what's going on dad? Mom, what's this about? Mama opens her mouth to speak but dad interrupts before she can get one word out. "I'm dying" dad yelled. "What? I said. RJ turns to me and says, "Did he just say he was dying? I said yes but I wanna know why you just blurt it out like that dad, I said, looking confused as ever. "Yeah, you didn't have to say it like that Rob", mom said speaking softly. "Well you tell them then", he said, acting all frustrated as if we offended him for what he did. "Well, I was going to start speaking until you interrupted me," mom said. She hated when he did that but under the circumstances, she was trying to remain calm. "Well, your dad has been sick for a while, he's had a spot on his lungs for about 2 years but now it's spread, and since he's refused treatment, it's gotten worse, it has metastasized all over his body". "Why didn't we know anything about this in the beginning," I said, didn't we have a right to know too? "Right, what right?" Dad yelled nobody has the right to tell me what to do with my body, nobody but the Lord. Dad, nobody wants to tell you what to do with your body, RJ said, we just would like to know what's going on with you and mama. "Ain't nothing wrong with me," my mama said sarcastically. "This ain't about you Diane" dad shouted! Goodness gracious, every time these kids get to talk to me or about me, you somehow insert yourself in the conversation!

Dad was mad. "Okay, okay, let's all calm down, mama, dad's right, this is not about you this time but dad, we still need an explanation on why you chose not to tell us about you having cancer. "I just explained it and I ain't explaining no more, He shouted. Now if the good Lord sees fit for me to leave this earth behind this disease then so be it. I don't want anybody worrying about me, nobody trying to fix me with all that chemo and needles and throwing up and stuff, I ain't having it. But dad, your decisions would still be your decisions, RJ said, we just want to be here to support and pray for you. Yes, dad, we could've been praying for you, I said, trying to hold back the tears. "Well, pray now, he said. Pray I have the strength to endure the 6 months they gave me and that I make it into the Kingdom of Heaven. I sat there for a minute, I couldn't believe what I just heard, then I looked up and said, Of course, we will dad, I said as I got up to give him a hug. But before I could wrap my arms around him, he said, "but that's not all I have to tell you, there's more", You might wanna sit back down for this one.

As he made this statement, he looked over at Jeff. I look at Jeff, then turn to look at RJ, he looks at Jeff then both RJ and I look at mama, what in the world does he have to do with this next announcement. My palms are sweaty now, I can't imagine what dad is getting ready to say. I remember sometime last year, I was in my prayer closet and the Holy Spirit led me to pray for my dad, I was fervently praying for his healing, so much so that I began to weep. I called dad that same day and asked him if he was doing alright and even though he sounded weak that day, he said he was doing fine, that he had been out in the yard and was just a little tired. I think back to that day, the Lord was trying to tell me that my dad was sick but I didn't pursue like I would normally do as an Intercessor, I guess I didn't want to know the truth, I pushed that moment in the back of my mind. I feel horrible about it now. Normally, I would have continued on in prayer and asked God for specifics and a prayer strategy because God often deals with me prophetically as well.

I wonder why I didn't. This is very disturbing and disappointing, to say the least. I could have known, I should have known. Lord give me the strength to walk through this journey, I feel so helpless right now. So, I go sit back down and look at Jeff, he doesn't look at me. He's looking guilty. I'm thinking, what the heck did he do? Did daddy make him the beneficiary of his estate, oh hell no, somebody better tell me what's up? I hated being in the dark about things, especially family matters. I was especially upset that Jeff knew what was going on and I couldn't understand why dad chose to confide in him. Well, I'm ready to hear what's next, at least I hope I'm ready, this is going to be a long night.

CHAPTER THREE

Surprise! Surprise!

Daddy just gave me the shock of my life! He just announced so casually that he has cancer and it's terminal. We didn't have time to grieve before he said that there was more to this story. What in the world could be worse than telling your family that you only have six more months to live? After I sat back down, I looked over and saw the tears running down mama's face.

I looked at RJ and his eyes were bugged out like he had a thyroid condition. We were all so stunned, even Jeff, at least he pretended to be. As I caught my breath, I asked daddy, "What else is going on? He then looked at mama, as if to question if she'd like to talk first. She nodded her head towards him, giving him the green light to proceed. He stands up, walks towards the window, turns, and says words I could not believe. "In light of the situation I'm facing, he says, considering that I only have six months to live and all, well, I'm getting ready to retire". He continues on saying, "I should have retired a long time ago but I was being stubborn, I just didn't want to sit down, I didn't want to give up the church but now I want to spend these last precious moments with your mother, with my children and grandchildren, I don't want or need the pressures of church business and preaching". Well, I can understand that dad, RJ said, I support you 100 percent. RJ got up and went to hug daddy, he then started crying which made me start crying even more. I stood up to go hug dad again but before I could get close, daddy said, "I'm handing the church over to Jeff, he's gonna be the senior pastor effective immediately". What? I screamed with a loud voice, what are you talking about? Jeff the Pastor, Jeff don't know nothing about pastoring daddy. I mean, yeah he's an associate minister but he barely knows the scripture, he ain't preached since last year, this is insane! I began pacing the floor, I did that when I got extremely upset. "Nadine calm down now!

My mama said, sit down and quit all that pacing, you gone wear my rug out". Mama, I ain't worried about no darn rug! I said. Watch your mouth young lady, she replied. And sit down and listen to your father. I went to sit down, but not by Jeff. I sat by Shannon of all people, she was the only person in the room who made any sense, mainly because she hadn't said a mumbling word so far. "Okay, now somebody explain to me how did Jeff get picked over all the other associate ministers?" I said, trying to stay calm. "What about Minister Brown, he's a great speaker or Reverend Gill, he's a good speaker too, Minister Parker, Evangelist Smith, gee dad so many ministers that are good speakers on the roster, why Jeff? What do you mean why Jeff? Jeff said with an angry tone. But before I could speak, "Jeff is the only one I can trust" dad said trying to reassure me of his decision. "He's a smart man Nadine, he'll learn how to do the preaching and stuff, he knows how to do the books and the legal matters and stuff, he's the one I want, I'm the pastor, it's my decision and I don't wanna hear nobody else's mouth about it now" dad shouted. I could see the tears streaming down his face. It was at that moment I realized just how scared he was. I walked towards him and gave him the biggest and longest hug, then mama came over, RJ, then Shannon, and yes, even Jeff. We all stood around daddy, hugging and crying and stuff, it became real emotional for a while.

I can't believe I let myself get all bent out of shape over Jeff taking over the church that I totally forgot the real reason why dad called us in for a meeting in the first place. I had to meditate on that moment for a minute. The fact that my parents knew all this time what dad had been going through and chose not to disclose any of this with me and RJ was very upsetting but I didn't want to seem selfish so I had to suppress my thoughts and focus on what was happening at this moment.

After a few minutes of crying, I wiped my face, went and sat down by my husband, put my hand on his knee, and asked, "Are you ready?" Ready as I'm gonna get, he said. Not quite the humbling answer I was expecting but okay. " I'm here to help you, babe, you have my support", I said. He looked at me for a second and said, "thank you. I feel like he knew I was lying, He knew that I was upset that he let daddy do this, he didn't even try to convince him otherwise. I felt like something else was going on but I couldn't put my finger on it. This was gonna be a mess!

The family continued on with the conversation about daddy's health, discussing what the doctors have said about how the cancer had spread and there was nothing else they could do since he refused to be treated. We briefly talked about how we were to announce daddy's retirement to the church but, daddy said he didn't want to discuss the terms of his will just yet. I thought that was strange because I knew that Jeff was the executor of his will, that I did know but daddy said we'll save that for another time. "Let's go eat", he said. We call all the kids downstairs and have dinner.

It was pretty quiet at the table, I guess we were all just trying to take everything in, no one is really making eye contact until RJ blurts out, "So Jeff, you ready to steer the ship?" Jeff looks up at him nervously and says, "well, I guess I'm ready, I mean it's truly an honor to be asked to step into pop's shoes. I'm sure he's going to teach me all that I need to know". I'm thinking to myself, dude, you could never wear my daddy's shoes, for one thing, your boat feet are way too big and so is your head, and another thing, did God ever call you to pastor? But I never say a word. As you can see, I do a lot of thinking in my head, things I say to myself that I probably would never say out loud. I guess that's my way of relieving some frustration or something, I don't know, I've been doing this since I was in the 3rd grade when I was being bullied by this fat girl named Paulette.

She always made fun of me but I was too scared to stand up for myself so I just talked smack in my head to get the fear and sometimes laugh out of my system. "So now you're going to be the 1st Lady Ms. Nadine", Shannon said with a touch of sarcasm in her voice. "Hmmm, I never thought about that, problem is, will mama relinquish her title?" I said laughing and looking at mama. Mama picked up her fancy glass full of iced tea, looked at me, and said, "I don't have a problem with passing the baton, I know Nadine can handle it". Well, that settles it, mama wasn't too cool with having to step down. How do I know? She called me Nadine. She always called me Nadine when she was unhappy with me about something. She called me Naddie all the other times. I adjust my seat and continue eating dinner, I look over next to me and notice

that daddy and Jeff are in a deep conversation, it sounded like they were talking about church stuff. Dad was explaining who he was going to introduce Jeff too, all the important people he needed to meet including some of his business partners, but what did that have to do with the church I wondered? I couldn't hear all that well because my nephew Chad was smacking so loud. His mama needs to really go get his teeth fixed, no ten-year-old boy should be chewing that way. I look over at RJ, he looks at me and gives me an eye signal to meet him in the kitchen. I get up first, making an excuse to go use the bathroom, 2 minutes later, RJ comes into the kitchen, he doesn't look happy at all. "So, what do you think about all this Naddie?" He said. "This is all too much to take in for one day, I mean dad is dying, refusing treatment and he acts like he's okay with all this." Then! RJ shouted, he has the nerve to assign Jeff of all people to head the church, something just ain't right Naddie,I mean I know that's your husband but it just doesn't make no sense to me". I walk towards my brother, I put my arm around him and say, "I'm with you bro, I don't understand it either but I guess we're going to have to deal with this the best way we can". We stood in the kitchen for a few more moments, tears rolling down our faces but quickly wiping them off so no one could tell that we had been crying. Crying was for wimps, dad would tell us that when we were kids.

It was like shedding tears was banned from our home. Daddy would get mad when we cried, he said God wanted us to be soldiers, he made us tough and strong like Michael the Archangel. Sometimes it seemed that dad was offended when we cried, I never understood that. He especially hated to see RJ crying, he called him a sissy one day when RJ accidentally cut his finger with the knife he was using trying to cut potatoes to make me some home-style French fries. Take told him to take it like a man and for me to wipe my tears too. He would say, "pain in a part of life, you don't have time to be crying about every little thing". That was embedded in us as kids, I guess that's why our reaction to his announcement about his health seemed so strange, we were too scared to cry. I was ready to cry more about Jeff being in charge than daddy's sickness, I cried more when I was angry as opposed to being hurt or sad.

We got ourselves together and walked back into the dining room. By this time, everyone was finished with dinner. Dad said to us, "I'm tired y'all, I need a nap". Mama asked if he wanted a piece of cake and a cup of coffee before his nap, he always liked that on a Sunday evening after dinner but he refused. He looked tired and weak but also concerned. So, I went over and gave him the biggest hug and kissed him on the lips, and said, "l love you daddy, I'm here if you need me". He said, "I know Nadine, I love you too." He let go of me real quick and walked out the room. He probably didn't want me to see him cry even though his voice shook when he was talking to me. I was hoping to see him shed a tear, then I would have felt okay to let go of all of my tears but he held it together, clearing his throat as he walked out the door of his study. RJ looked up and noticed he was leaving. "Dad, dad", he shouted, trying to get dad's attention. RJ walked out of the room and followed dad upstairs. I wonder what he's going to say to him. Jeff was looking and probably wondering the same thing. I know he wishes he could be a fly on the wall. "Naddie, let me talk to you for a minute," Said mama, as she gently placed her napkin on the table. She motioned for me to meet her in the sunroom; that was her favorite place to sit, meditate and read. "Okay mama," I said, looking perplexed. RJ wants to talk to dad, mama wants to talk to me, all these secret meetings would make anyone uncomfortable. I wonder what Jeff is thinking?

I wonder what Shannon is thinking? I wonder if they will start a conversation of their own while we're away. My stomach is in knots! I wish I could start this day over. I'm ready to go home, I miss Rollo, he always comforts me, he likes to sit in my lap and be rubbed and I love rubbing on him when I'm in deep thought. I proceed to follow mama to the sunroom, all I could think is what she could want to talk to me about in private and what do I say if Jeff asks me what we talked about. Do I tell him or keep it from him in spite, I don't know? What I do know is that it's going to be a long ride home.

After the dust settled some and RJ returned to the study briefly just to tell Shannon that he'd be a little while longer talking to dad and that if she was ready to go home he'd have dad's driver Mr. Ernest take them home. Everyone was ready to leave. RJ told me that he would call me later so I hug him and Shannon and grab my things to meet Jeff in the car. RJ went back to wherever he left dad waiting. Jeff stayed back gathering some documents, probably trying to buy some time and wait until RJ leaves so he can try and find out what he and dad discussed. I guess they were taking too long because I saw him walking out the front door, looking sweaty and nervous. Once he got in the car, there was a big old elephant that followed him in there.

Neither one of us knew what to say so he just apologized to me about dad. He said he was sorry this was happening and that he wished that dad would have gotten the chemo and radiation like the doctors recommended. I told him that I was still in shock and couldn't find the words to express myself at the moment. He let me have my peace and simply turned on some smooth jazz and allowed me to meditate on my feelings. I didn't feel like talking, especially not to him and I think he sensed it. I feel sick, my head is hurting and my heart is pounding out of my chest. I haven't felt this way since I had pneumonia years ago. I don't know what's wrong, maybe it's my anxiety? It's been a long, strange day, I'm ready to go home and pop one of my anxiety pills and get some rest. Tomorrow probably won't get any better.

CHAPTER FOUR

Life Changes

It's Monday morning, I didn't sleep well at all last night, and I don't think Jeff did either. That anxiety pill I took didn't help at all. We both tossed and turned like a ship in a hurricane. I'm not surprised though, we didn't do much talking on the drive home from my parent's house last night. Jeff didn't even ask me what me and mama talked about, he only mentioned dad's health once then we listened to the radio for the rest of the way home. I didn't get a chance to ask RJ what he and dad talked about because they were still in the room talking when Jeff and I left.

I still have a headache, I'm calling in sick today. I mean, I can deal with this minor headache but I've got too much on my mind to be dealing with doctors, nurses and patients. I see Jeff is already gone, his side of the bed is empty, as usual. I'm kind of glad though, I need some time to myself. I get up to wash my face and brush my teeth. I hear Rollo barking downstairs, I'm wondering why and why he hasn't ran up here yet like he normally does. I go downstairs and to my surprise, Jeff is sitting at the kitchen table. "Good morning, I thought you were gone", I said as I tapped him on his shoulder.

He's on his laptop working, he responds by saying, "Good morning, I think me and you should talk". I said okay but then looked over to see Rollo tied up to a chair. "Why is he tied up, did you let him out this morning?" I asked him as I untied Rollo. "He was getting on my nerves jumping all over the place, I told him to go upstairs but he didn't so I tied him up". I looked over at his doggy tray and noticed he had no water or no food. "That's what is wrong with mama's baby, he's hungry". I said as I let him loose and gave him a hug. I quickly feed Rollo and then sit down at the table with Jeff. "Okay, let's talk", I said, eager to hear what he has to say. He closes his laptop and puts it in his bag then says, "I just want to know how you feel about everything, I mean I'm sure it's upsetting to hear about your dad having cancer, that's a given and I'm very sad to know he's going through all of that but I'm talking about his decision to make me the senior pastor, you didn't seem too comfortable with that last night".

I lean over to look at Rollo, making sure he ate all his food so I can let him back outside. He's lying on the floor listening to our conversation like he knows this could get good. "I told you that I'm here to support you, Jeff, I meant that but honestly, I am a little shocked, no offense to you but I just wasn't expecting all this" Jeff stands up to put on his jacket, he's already ready to leave, then he says, "I just want you to know that I will do everything in my power to keep pop's legacy alive, I want you to help me do that Nadine, I'm gonna need your support". You have my support babe, I'm glad to hear you say that, that makes me feel better.

I'm still trying to take this all in, I don't think it has really hit me yet, I mean yeah the church stuff is surprising but I'm just now realizing that my dad is dying". Jeff walks over to me and wraps his arms around me, it's been a long time since I've felt his arms like this, it felt good and he smelled good. I leaned in a little more, tilting my head hoping he would lean in for a kiss, he does but only on my forehead! I pull back as he lets me go. "I've gotta get going, I have a meeting with a client and then have a meeting with pops, he's introducing me to some people tonight, some trustees or something. "Oh so, he's ready to tell people already, I thought he was waiting to make the announcement at the church on Sunday" I asked. "He is, said Jeff, I guess this is an informal meeting, he said to get my feet wet". Dad had decided during our family meeting that he would make an announcement to the church about his retirement next Sunday, he didn't feel it necessary to prolong things any longer. "Yea good old pops, even during this sad occasion, he still finds a way to make me laugh" Jeff chuckles as he walks out the door. I grab Rollo's leash and walk behind him. I need to take him for a walk so he won't potty on my floor, he never really did that though, only when Brandon came home, as if he was marking his territory or something. Speaking of Brandon, I need to call him. He called me last night but didn't leave a message, he always called on Sunday's so I better call him before he gets his day started.

After Rollo and I return from our walk, I call Brandon to check up on him. "Hey mama, he said as he answered the phone after one ring. Hey son, I saw you called me last night but we were at your grandparents for dinner and I had my phone on silent, how are you? He said, "I'm good mama, what was the special occasion, it's been a while since I remember you going over there for dinner, especially on a Sunday. You always told me you'd had enough of grandma and grandpa during church and you like to unwind at home. I told Brandon it was just something RJ wanted to do since we hadn't spent time together in a while. He was even more shocked to know that RJ and his family were there too. Wow! He said, I missed all the fun, I hope I get to see everyone when I get to come home next week. "You're coming home, that's great when?

I shouted, with excitement in my voice. I wanted to surprise you, he said, but it's good I'm telling you now since you wanna go visiting and stuff. We talked for a few minutes, catching up and making each other laugh, then Brandon said, "Wait a minute, are you home, what are you doing home, why are you not at work? I guess he heard Rollo barking at a bird outside in the background. Yeah, I said, I took off today, I have a headache and now my stomach is bothering me, I'm getting ready to go lay back down. It must be grandma's cooking, he laughed. "Oh, by the way, I talked to Brittany yesterday, she said she's going to San Francisco for some job interview. Oh really, I said. I hardly get a chance to talk to her, every time I call, she be rushing me off the phone, I said with a sad voice. You know how Brittany is mom, she's always busy, he said.

I knew he was just trying to comfort me, he knew that Brittany and I weren't that close, she was more like a daddy's girl, in fact, she was like her father in more ways than one, I guess that's why we bumped heads so much. I loved her though, she was my baby girl but she always made me feel like she never liked me, I wonder where I went wrong. Nevertheless, Brandon and I were like peas in a pod, we looked out for one another. "Let's get back to you mama", Brandon said, changing the subject from Brittany so I won't get too deep in my feelings. "Are you sure you're okay, I mean you rarely get sick, at least not so sick to where you call off work". "Yea, son, I'm fine, I say, honestly, I'm just tired, I need to catch up on some sleep, I've been so busy working at the hospital and at church, I'm probably just sleep deprived. I started to think to myself that Brandon was right, it was strange for me to be taking off of work, I was so busy worrying over dad's health and this church business that I hadn't even thought twice about how I was feeling. In all honesty, I haven't been myself in a while. These on and off headaches and fatigue have been happening for a few weeks, now I'm beginning to feel sick in my stomach, I wonder if I have some kind of virus? Well, I'll make an appointment to get a check- up soon.

After a few more jokes with Brandon, hearing him talk about his relationship with his girlfriend Gina, whom I've yet to meet. We give each other telephone hugs and kisses, tell each other how much we love one another and that we're still best friends, my heart melts, I blew one last kiss then I got off the phone with Brandon, anticipating his visit next week but still a little shaken from all the surprise announcements that took place last night. I wasn't prepared to tell Brandon about his grandpa nor about his father becoming the new church pastor, I don't know how he's going to take all that, he sounded so happy on the phone, I didn't want to take that from him, at least not yet.

I grabbed a cup of coffee and returned upstairs to my bedroom, Rollo followed me and quickly jumped in my bed but I wanted to sit in my bay window, one of my favorite spots. I looked out the window just to see all the people in the neighborhood busy with their day; adults going off to work and kids headed off to school, it was a normal Monday morning, but not for me. I had so many thoughts going on in my brain, especially the private conversation I had with mama right before Jeff and I left last night. Mama told me that I needed to be strong for daddy and that he has been sick for a long time. She said she tried and tried to get daddy to agree to treatment, even after he refused chemotherapy, she suggested a more holistic and natural treatment but, he still refused.

She said he had been in a lot of pain and she thinks he's getting tired, almost like he's ready to die, but the one thing that shocked me the most at that moment is when she said, "Naddie, I'm scared. I know yall think I'm a strong woman, and I am for the most part, but life as I know it, the 46 years I've been with your father, it's all going to be over, all will be different". I almost broke down again just thinking about her words. I could hear and almost feel the love she had for daddy, I could feel the pain of her heart breaking. I have never seen my mama like that. I've always known her to be such a strong person, rarely showing her emotions. I've seen her so happy, like when daddy first bought her that big ol' house or when she got so angry when a woman at church accused daddy of trying to hit on her at the church picnic one year but I've never seen her this sad, this heartbroken. It almost seemed like her heart was breaking for more than one reason though, but what else could be so devastating than losing the man that you love?

Mama was loving but stoic, so much so that she made me wipe the tears from my eyes before I left the sun room with her last night. She said, "now dry your tears my dear, I'm gonna be alright and you are too, just remember, us women are the backbone of our families and we will never let anyone take that away from us".

I often wonder where my mama got her strength from. Could it have been her mom? I would never know because I never met her, she died before I was born. All I know about her is the pictures mama has in her photo albums, she looks just like mama's sister Ida. Aunt Lucille, mama's oldest sister said that aunt Ida was just like their mama, pretty as a butterfly but crazy as a bessie bug. I liked her though, she always made me laugh by telling dirty jokes. Aunt Lucille was in a nursing home, she suffered from multiple sclerosis and could no longer walk or care for herself. Her children threw her in a nursing home and took over her house, it's a shame too because they tore that house up. Half of them ended up on drugs so they rarely even visit Aunt Lucille, with her living in California, mama can only go visit her a few times a year. Mama takes care of her expenses because if it were up to those crazy kids of hers, she'd already be six feet under. It's so embarrassing to have cousins that will do that to their mom, she was all they had after their father ran off and left, chasing that crack pipe.

I guess that's where they inherited their addictions from. I make it a point not to answer any of their calls because they are always asking for money. My Aunt Ida lives in Germany, she married an army Colonel and he's stationed at USAG Baumholder Army Base in Baumholder, Germany, so she lives over there with him. She never had any kids, rumor has it that she got "fixed" when she was dating this white man who promised to marry her but he said he didn't want any kids. Needless to say, that didn't work, he left her and she bought a cat. Every time I think about that story I crack up laughing because Ida went a little coo-coo for Cocoa Puffs after that fiasco. After mama went to Texas to straighten her out, she met her now-husband at Fort Hood army base where she worked in the hospital, they dated for years before he decided to marry her, now they live overseas and she's been happier than I've ever seen her before. I don't know what mama did but whatever it was, it worked.

I found myself smiling and laughing while sitting in that bay window, reminiscing on good times yet, pondering over the bad. Things are really going to be different from now on. Just the thought of not being able to see my daddy preach his Sunday morning services brings tears to my eyes, and the thought of having to watch Jeff do it brings pain to my side. Oh Lord! What am I to do? I'm starting to feel overwhelmed, I decided to take a shower to unwind, I don't plan on doing anything today, I just wanna sleep, I'm too exhausted to be nosey and harass Jeff about his meeting with daddy. My brain needs a break!

I jumped in the shower, got my smooth jazz playing, Rollo on the carpet acting like a pervert, staring at me while I'm naked. As I begin to wash my body, rubbing my hands over my breast, I feel a small knot in my left breast. "Wait a minute", I say out loud. Rollo sits up as if I'm talking to him. "What is this I'm feeling?" It kinda feels like a little marble. I shake it off, as a nurse, I know we women have a lot of milk ducts, fatty tissue, and lymph nodes in the breast area, I'm thinking maybe it's just swollen or clogged, it doesn't hurt. I don't want to think of anything else, I refuse to add more stress in my life but there are a thousand what if's in the back of my mind. I continue to shower and begin to sing some of my favorite worship songs, if there was ever a time I needed the Lord, I sure did need him now. I have to get it together, save the emotions and worry for another day, your daddy needs you, your mama needs you, I say to myself. Take one crisis at a time, is all I keep saying in my head but I know better. I know that this lump needs to be attended to, I know when I looked in the mirror, my breast didn't look the same. My left breast looks a bit swollen and dimply as opposed to the right breast. I do another self-examination and could clearly tell the difference between the left and the right. I know what it could be but I'm not ready to hear it. I suppress it, choosing not to tell anyone anything until I find out and right now, I don't want to know. I couldn't handle any more bad news, I'm acting just like my daddy. Maybe this is what he went through and why he chose not to say anything to the family. I haven't even been diagnosed yet and I'm already scared and bombarding my mind with thoughts. I lay in bed and cry myself to sleep, I'm crying over so many things it's driving me crazy. Where is God? I need so many answers, why is all this happening to me?

Hours later, I wake up from my nap, it's 2:00! I yelled to myself, boy I must have been tired, I wasn't expecting to sleep this long, almost 6 hours. Perhaps that anxiety pill finally kicked in. I needed that nap though, with getting very little sleep last night and all the stress I'm taking in, my body is now responding to that. Speaking of my body, I get up to look in the mirror once more. I'm inspecting this area on my breast where I felt the lump. "I better call Dr.Ho, I need to see her asap". Dr.Ho was my family practitioner, a great doctor indeed, she's been my physician for years, she's needed to put in a referral for me to get a mammogram. I had a change of heart about knowing right away what is going on with my body.

I refuse to take my family through what RJ and I experienced. I have to be careful though; I don't want to overload my parents with bad news. "Wait a minute, what am I thinking?" I say as I wash my face again with cold water. I'm acting like I already know what's going on. I mean as a nurse who has previously worked in the Breast Center Clinics, I know the signs but why have I pronounced this over myself? God can change the report, He can heal me now if I chose to believe. Do I have it in me to stretch my faith? Is this all a part of God's plan? If so, I know he will help me endure yet I already feel so helpless. I need to go on a fast, I need to hear God clearly and I'm gonna need his strength to help me get through this season of my life. I get on the side of my bed and start praying, talking to God was so comforting to me and boy do I have a lot to talk about. I'm headed down an unfamiliar path and I'm surely going to need the Lord to walk with me.

CHAPTER FIVE

The Heavy Weights

A couple of weeks went by and I was finally able to get in to see Dr. Ho, she immediately scheduled my mammogram and put a rush on my biopsy as a favor to me because we've known each other for years. Yes, I, like my father, have cancer. Stage 2B breast cancer is what I've been diagnosed with. I still can't seem to wrap my mind around all of this. I've been tested, had a biopsy, and gotten my results in a matter of 10 days. The sad thing is that I went through all of this alone. I was going to take Brandon with me and tell him everything but he had to reschedule his trip home due to some event the radio station was hosting, but he said he'll be home this weekend, he promised. I hadn't talked to Jeff about any of this. He's been too busy frolicking in dad's footsteps ever since dad made the announcement to the church and so many people support his decision to make Jeff the senior pastor. Though Jeff has noticed something different. He's been asking me if I'm okay and said that I seemed a little distant. He's probably thinking that my mood change has something to do with him but it doesn't. Right now, being mad at my dad and Jeff is the last thing on my mind.

Honestly, I haven't even thought much about my dad's sickness on the count of my own devastating news. I've got to tell my family soon, this is all too much for me to handle alone. I feel bad for not telling Jeff, after all, he is my husband but honestly, I am scared of his reaction. I'm afraid he might not care enough about me having cancer than my dad. I wanted to tell him but not more than I wanted to tell my son. Brandon had become my true confidant. Over the years, we have confided in one another about relationships, insecurities, and challenges. He's seen me go through a lot and I have prayed for him through many situations and bad decisions. I can't wait until he gets home. Meanwhile, I have to figure out a way to tell Jeff and the rest of the family. I'm hoping he and Brittany will show the same compassion towards me as they did my dad, time will tell.

I've been going to work still, I don't want to make any sudden changes in my routine until I've talked to my family. Today is Thursday, I went shopping on my way home from work. I had to get some of Brandon's favorite things so I could make him a good home-cooked meal. As I sit down to rest a bit, I hear the front door open and a voice talking in the distance, I walk around the corner and to my surprise it's Brittany. Hey! I said, as she walked in and sat her luggage at the front door. She waves at me because she's on the phone and I guess saying hello is out of the question. I stand there for a second and she comes over to give me a hug then she walks into her dad's office and closes the door. I guess this is a very important phone call, so I go back to the kitchen wondering what she's doing here and why she hadn't called to tell me she was coming. I'm feeling exhausted but can't let her see me like this, I drink a cup of water, and then she pops in the kitchen saying, "well hello mom, it's good to see you". I turn and give her another hug, she feels frail, "have you been eating, you feel like a skeleton Brittany", I say to her as I look her up and down. "What are you doing here?" I had no idea you were coming. "Well, I decided to stop in for a quick visit, I'm on my way back from San Francisco, I've got some exciting news, is dad home?" She opens the refrigerator to see if I'd bought something that she actually eats. "No, your dad hasn't made it home yet, what's the exciting news? I want to tell the both of you whenever he gets here, I'm so excited I could scream!" She grabs her phone and heads up to her old bedroom, leaving her luggage behind expecting me to bring it to her. I'm glad to see her but find it strange that she randomly popped up. She didn't spend much time with me, but I never expect her to, we were never really close. I don't know what I did or what I said to make her so distant from me, she's just always been her daddy's baby. Well, I'll find my comfort tomorrow when Brandon gets here. I planned to tell him about my diagnosis and everything else that's going on but now I have to tell Brittany and Jeff too. I'm so not ready for all of this, the scary thing is that I'm not sure how they all will respond.

I guess I won't see Brit until her dad comes home because she grabbed an apple and made her way to her old bedroom, meanwhile, I'll start prepping my dinner for tomorrow, Brandon loved great northern beans and cornbread, I'm gonna put the beans in the crockpot with some smoked turkey then order some take out for today, I don't have the energy to cook twice.

An hour later, I hear Brittany running down the stairs, she breaks her neck getting to the door and Jeff barely can make it inside before she jumps around his neck and gives him all kinds of hugs and kisses. She didn't do that for me but I quit expecting that from her years ago. "Daddy, I got some good news to tell you, she said as she grabs his hand leading him to the dining room table. Jeff looks at me and says, "Hey baby, what's all this about? "I don't know she wouldn't tell me anything until you came home". Well, says Brittany, I've just secured a great job at the Walden & Walden law firm in San Francisco, I'm moving there next month, I'm so excited, I always wanted to live in California. "Congratulations! Jeff and I shouted at the same time but I said, "When did you pass the bar, I didn't even know you took the test?" Oh mama, I took the bar 4 months ago, I got my results 2 weeks ago that's when I went to San Fran for my interview and nailed this job, it's my dream job! I originally planned to go in as an apprentice because I wasn't sure I was going to pass but I did! She shouted as she continued to jump up and down with excitement. So Jeff and Brittany start talking, I walk back into the kitchen and all I can think about is why Jeff knew about her passing the bar and why was she telling me that she was studying the times I called her? My feelings are so hurt, I can't let this go. I have to address it, "Brittany, I yelled, come here for a second.

I can just imagine her eyes rolling as she got up from the table to walk into the kitchen. Yes, she says with a little attitude in her voice. "Why didn't you tell me you passed the bar, that's something I would have liked to know too, I'm proud of you too". "I'm sorry mama, I told dad to tell you, I guess he got busy…" Mmmmm, I guess so, he does have a lot of new responsibilities now" I said, sarcastically not realizing I almost let the cat out of the bag. What responsibilities does he have, dad, she shouted as she walked back into the dining room, do you have a new job or something, what is mama talking about? She looks upset as if she's mad that her dad has kept something from her. I ran in behind her to let her know that dad and I will be talking to her and Brandon tomorrow about something. "Brandon is coming home, what? What's going on?

Immediately after Brittany bombards me with questions, Brandon comes walking through the door. Hey! Hey! Anybody home, Brandon yells as he dumps his duffle bag on the floor. I drop everything and run to him and wrap my arms so tight around his body. I could feel the ugly stares from Jeff and Brittany.

They both always envied how close me and my son are, even though they have the same kind of relationship with one another. I guess because I seem so happy when Brandon is around. Brandon is so surprised to see Brittany, he picks her up and swings her around then gives his dad some dap, smirking as he says, "What's up pop?" Brit Brit, what are you doing here, girl I haven't seen you in a minute. He says, staring her up and down as if he wants to give her a sandwich. Girl, what have you been eating? Or better yet, what have you not been eating, why are you so skinny? Boy! First of all I'm not skinny, I'm slim and I've been a vegetarian for almost a year now so I'm a lot healthier these days too.

Then Jeff intervenes, “Yea, the stress of taking the bar and passing it first try didn't help either. What! You passed, Brandon yelled while giving his sister a high five, congratulations Brit! Well, I’m glad to know that I wasn’t the only one who didn’t know until today, I said sarcastically. Jeff gives me the evil eye as to say, don’t start no mess. So I quickly return to the kitchen, I’m gonna cook all your favorites Bran, I yell from the kitchen. Brit, you’re gonna have to let me know what you eat now that you’re vegan. I'm a vegetarian mom, she says with an annoyed tone, vegan and vegetarian are 2 different things. Of course I knew that, I just wanted to get a rise out of her since she left me out of her good news.

I need to stop being petty. There’s so much to talk about and wrap my mind around. I’m so glad to be cooking, it’s almost like therapy for me at times. Brandon comes in, peaking at every pot on the stove. So mama, what’s been up with you? You must be working too hard, you have dark circles under your eyes, is it work, church, or pops getting on your nerves, he says while chuckling under his voice. All three, I say laughing but knowing it’s true. I’m thinking that I need to have a conversation with my family after dinner. I hate to spoil the excitement but I need to get this over with and I especially want to break the news to my children before we head over to Mamas. Lord give me the strength to make it through this storm that lies ahead.

After having dinner with the family, I summoned everyone into the family room to let them know about what has been going on. Well, kids, I say softly, I have some news to tell you, some good news and some bad, which do you want first? But before they could say their preference, Jeff yells out, “let me tell them babe.” Well, he says while partly smirking, “I am going to be the new Senior Pastor of Grace Christian Center real soon”. What? They both said. Even Brittany seemed surprised, “why are You going to be the pastor, is grandpa stepping down or what”, she said. Yeah, what brought this on? “Is something wrong with grandpa?”, said Brandon, as he looked concerned and confused. I interjected, “Pastor has taken ill and he wants to rest. I hesitated thinking the kids would say something but they just sat there looking stunned. I continued on, "guys, grandpa has cancer, lung cancer and he only has about 6-12 months to live based on what the doctors have said. Brittany immediately began to cry, Brandon just sat there, staring off into space saying he can't believe it. I go and sit next to Brittany and hug her, surprisingly she begins to hug me back. She laid her head on my shoulder and cried like a baby and kept telling me she was so sorry. The moment was bittersweet. I was sad because she was so distraught but it felt nice to hug her and the fact that she allowed me to was a beautiful moment. It had been a long time since I held my baby girl like this. I think she was in the 8th grade the last time she allowed me to love on her in this way, that was when the boy she wanted to go to the 8th grade dance with actually asked her best friend to go and she went, knowing that Brittany was in love with him. I'll never forget Darryl Spencer, I wanted to break his neck for breaking my baby's heart. And Michelle Lee, some best friend, I never let her spend another night over here after she did what she did to Brittany but somehow, after that, Brit turned on me, said I made her friend turn against her. She couldn't see at the time that Michelle was never her best friend.

All I wanted to do was protect her, just like I do now. I want to protect her from the pain she's feeling about her grandpa. Suddenly, she breaks away from me and gets up and goes to her dad, she lays her head on his chest and continues crying. Brandon comes over to me and grabs my hand. "Mama, are you okay?" he says as tears roll down his face. Yes, baby, I'm fine now, I've had some time to take this all in, now I need to be strong for dad and mama too. How about you, are you alright, I know this is shocking news. He says, yes ma'am, I just can't believe it. I never thought someone as strong as grandpa would be going through this. I just don't understand, that man is in love with the Lord, how could God allow this to happen to him? Him of all people? Brandon began to cry, I just grabbed my son and held him telling him it wasn't God's fault. This was not God punishing my dad. Some things in life we just can't explain Brandon, I said as I wiped the tears from his face. Grandpa has had a good life, a very good life. He's done great work for God's kingdom and now God wants him to continue that work in heaven. That's the only way I can explain it son. After that, we all sat around for hours reliving great memories of my parents and how I grew up, and how they loved the kids.

It ended up being a wonderful night, a night I would have never expected under the circumstances. Somehow that news about my dad brought my own family a bit closer, even if it were for only one night. I did not have it in me to end the night with more bad news about my own cancer diagnoses, I just couldn't bring myself to tell any of them. I guess I was being selfish, selfish in a way that I didn't want to talk about my health issues, I only wanted to love on my husband and my twins. This bond was something I had not felt in a very long time, I guess I wanted to bask in the glow of all this love. I made the decision to tell everyone all at once. When we get to my parent's house after church on Sunday, everyone will know.

I have to tell them, I can't hide it any longer because I'll be scheduled for surgery soon as well as chemo and radiation. As for now, I'm loving what I'm seeing, my husband, sitting next to me with his arm around me, my twins sitting next to one another holding hands. This is the love that I miss, I wish I could stay here forever. I'll keep this day etched in the back of my heart always.

Finally, it's Sunday afternoon and we all convene at my parent's house, well at least me and my family because Robert said he couldn't make it because Shannon wasn't feeling well, she has a cold or something but I think he's not ready to face dad again and he's still a little pissed that Jeff has been named the new pastor of the church even though he has absolutely no interest in being the pastor himself. He has no idea that I'm about to make this announcement. Me and my family walk in greeting my parents. "It's so good to see yall" mom said as she hugged both of the twins. Come in, come in she said as she grabbed Brittany's hand leading her into the family room where dad was. Brandon walked past them real fast trying to get to dad before they did, he stood behind the chair, leaned over, and whispered softly, "What's going on old man?" Old man! Dad said as he stood straight up, wearing his smoker's jacket, looking relaxed. I got your old man, he said as he reached out to Brandon and gave him the biggest hug.

My parents love my children so much, they always spoil them no matter how old they get. As we all sit down, I notice the twins looking scared, they don't know what to say at this moment so my mom steps up and starts the conversation. Well, it was a wonderful surprise seeing yall as you walked through the doors of the church. Your mama didn't tell me y'all were in town, what's the occasion? I just came to visit them, Brittany said, I had no idea Brandon was coming. Tell her the good news Brit, Jeff said while cheesing like a Cheshire cat. He took pride in her achievements as if he had done them himself. "I passed the bar!" She said excitedly, I passed and have been offered a great job in San Francisco. "That's wonderful, my mom said, I'm so happy for you. Yea, finally some good news around here, said dad as he pulls out his pipe and places it in the corner of his mouth. "Pops what are you doing? " Jeff blurts out, since when did you start smoking a pipe?

He been smoking pipes, he never stopped, mama said. He lied and said he did but he didn't. Well I don't smoke no more, dad said in a sarcastic manner, all this woman let me do is put the pipe in my mouth, ain't no tobacco in it! Brandon busts out laughing, realizing the same thing I'm thinking, what's the point? After 2 or 3 more minutes of small talk, I was ready to have this conversation. I wanted dad to know that the kids knew what was going on. "Dad, mama, I told the twins about dad's condition last night, so we don't have to ignore the elephant in the room, they already know. Yea, I'm so sorry Papa, said Brittany as she goes to him and hugs him. Yea, me too big guy, I'm sorry to hear the news, is there anything I can, I mean we can do? Brandon said while grabbing dad's hand? Yea, go get me some tobacco to put in this here pipe, dad says while laughing. We all began to laugh but if I know my dad correctly, he was serious. While we were laughing, dad blurts out, hell, you might as well, I'm dying anyway, might as well die happy. Rob! My mom yells, stop saying that! Well, it's true Nadine, might as well face it, he says as he sits the pipe on the table next to him and sips his tea. Dad, you don't have to keep reminding us, I tell him as I shift and sit up in my seat because I'm ready to release my own secret.

(Cough cough) I have an announcement myself, I said in a loud voice, trying to get everyone's attention. The room gets quiet, everyone is looking at me like I stole something, I'm nervous as hell but I have to say it. Well, I know dad's announcement about his terminal cancer diagnosis has been a shock to everyone, I'm still trying to wrap my head around it. At first, I could not understand why dad chose to keep this information from us, he didn't want us to worry and he needed time to reconcile with himself about what he is facing. I can understand that fully now because I recently found out that I too have cancer, breast cancer and I'm gonna be having surgery real soon. Suddenly, all I could hear was chatter in the room, Jeff looked stunned, the twins looked scared, my parents looked confused, everyone started bombarding me with questions all at once, I was overwhelmed and just screamed, Hold It!!!! Wait one minute, I can only answer one question at a time so let me eliminate the confusion and tell you all what's going on.

I found out about my diagnosis shortly after dad told us about his. With everything going on, the changes in the church, dad's health and stuff, I couldn't find the right time to tell anyone. Not even me? Jeff said sadly, not even me, your own mother? My mom started with tears in her eyes, no not anybody, I'm so sorry, I'm so sorry to be telling you guys this with all that dad is going through, I just needed you all to know because I'm scared, I need yall support too but I don't want to take away from what dad is dealing with. "You don't owe nobody no explanation Nadine! Dad said in a stern voice. Stop apologizing, this is YOU, your body, your situation, it has nothing to do with me and mine. My destiny has already been spoken, and just because my time is winding down don't mean yours is. What are the doctors saying? Well, they say I'm at stage 2 dad, 2B and I've chosen to have a full mastectomy because, well you know, the family history and everything. So you're going to get both breasts removed Naddie, mama asked, are you sure you want to do that? Yes ma'am, I'm sure, I don't wanna take no chances and relapse. Brandon stands up and comes to hug me, mama are you sure you gonna be okay?

He starts crying and hugging me real tight. Yea, baby, I'll be fine, don't worry, God's got me. Brittany comes to give me a hug and kiss, mama, I just don't know what to say, she says, looking surprised and guilty for whatever reason. Maybe her guilt is because she doesn't know how to feel right now but she's trying to show me some love. I sit the twins down, and go and sit by Jeff, I hold his hand and say, "I know this is a lot to take in, dad's situation and now mine, it's hard but not impossible. I'm so sorry that I didn't tell you, I wanted to but I had a hard time accepting all of this myself. I apologize for not discussing the mastectomy with you, I just didn't want anyone to change my mind. This is the time for us to pull together and support one another. "I understand Nadine, I just wish you would have told me, you should not have to go through all of that alone. He then grabbed my hand and kissed it. He just sat there looking shocked, he couldn't put his words together anymore. I looked at my dad and said, "Dad, I'm still going to be here for you and love on you as much as I can, I believe we still have time right?" He looks at me as tears stream down his face and says, Naddie, I love you, always remember that. You be sure to carry that love with you no matter what. I stood up to embrace him, he was being so strong for me, forgetting about his own illness to love on me, the moment was priceless.

As for mama, she still looked stunned, for the first time in a long time, she didn't have much to say. She hopped up and said, I need to call your brother, have you told RJ? She asked as she walked out of the room. No ma'am I haven't talked to him about it yet, I yelled. I was talking to the back of her head, I looked at dad as to say, what's going on? Why won't she look at me? It seemed like he could read my thoughts. He said, give her some time Naddie, this is a lot for her to deal with. Dealing with me and my hard-headed self, now you, that's your mother, she's scared and she's hurting, you understand, don't you? Yes, sir I do, I understand. We all sat there for another hour or so talking, the kids alternating hugs between me and dad and Jeff stroking my hair from time to time, it was nice but mama never came back in the room. I could hear her talking on the phone perhaps to RJ, I don't know? But she was whispering a lot so I decided that it was time to leave. I knocked on her bedroom door but she never answered. I guess I needed to give her time to process all of this. Mama was never good at communicating when she was hurt so I decided to leave her alone.

I was ready to get home, my head was hurting and I still needed to finish dinner. I planned on frying some chicken to go with the beans and cornbread I made yesterday but Jeff thought it would be better for us to grab some chicken on the way home, I'm glad he did because I was mentally exhausted. This was going to be a long road ahead and I just wanted to be around my kids so we spent the night as a family snuggled in our theater room with cozy blankets and snacks watching movies. Well, I was watching them for the first time and I don't know how long, my family was together, all getting along and enjoying one another's company for more than one day. It was great to see Brandon and Brit laying head to head watching movies like they did when they were little and

It was especially nice to lay snug under Jeff with his arm around me. He pretended to be watching the movie too but I could tell he was deep in thought. I often wondered what was on his mind, time would only tell, I don't want to think too much about it, just enjoy this moment and feel the love that exuded through the room.

CHAPTER SIX

Nadine Needs a Nurse

Over the past six weeks, I have been able to spend time with my kids during their short visit and finish up some paperwork at my job before I took my medical leave. The word got out at church that I too was battling cancer and I spent the last few Sundays running from aunt Ruby and all the other nosey roseys in the church. Everyone is trying to find out more details about me and daddy's business and wondering why Jeff hasn't preached yet though dad had a special ceremony to make it official that Jeff is senior pastor. A host of guest speakers and pastors have come to preach and the congregation is wondering what's going on. Jeff made an announcement that he has postponed his 1st official sermon as senior pastor until after my surgery because he wants me to be there with him when he brings forth his message as the official Senior pastor but I think the joker is scared. He knows he's out of his league and could never really fill dad's shoes. Since the ceremony, a few members have left Grace Christian Center because they don't want to be pastored by Jeff and they have been loyal to my dad.

They don't understand that this is dad's doing but if they chose to leave, they were only committed to my dad, not to the church as a whole, and most likely not to God. A bunch of the assisting ministers have been side-eyeing Jeff and blaming his position on nepotism. They act like they can't wait until the day he stands before the congregation to preach, all hoping he chokes and falls dead. It's a shame but I can understand their concern. Jeff was one of many assisting pastors at the church but only ministered a handful of times over the course of 10 years. He was mainly involved in the legal and financial matters of the church. Though I wasn't an associate minister in the beginning, I did get ordained and licensed right after Jeff did and I'm still a little upset by what dad did by handing him the torch, He didn't even consider me and I'm his daughter, I'm anointed for this. Dad was old school though, he felt some type of way about women preaching. It took him a while to come to terms with women in the pulpit but he still didn't believe in a woman pastoring. Nevertheless, I pray that God will intervene and help Jeff lead his people right, after all, I will be the new first lady and my reputation is on the line as well.

All this time has passed by, I had my mastectomy and immediate reconstructive surgery and recovered well, praising God. Today I'm on my way home from the hospital. My doctor kept me in the hospital for 3 days because my blood pressure was too high. I'm so happy to be going home and get in my own bed. Brandon came home for my surgery but Brittany did not. She said her new job would not give her the time off from work because she's on a 90 day probation period but I felt like she still could have come home for the weekend or something. She did call me a few times while I was in the hospital, the conversations were rushed but she did tell me she loved me and I guess that's all that matters right now. As for Jeff, well, he was there for the surgery and came to the hospital every day to check on me but today, he's been M.I.A. (missing in action) so this is the reason why Brandon is bringing me home. Jeff called me at the hospital and said he had a very important meeting at the church and he asked Brandon to take me home. I spoke to my dad and asked about the meeting, he said he knew nothing of it. My dad was sounding weaker, he did more coughing than talking when I spoke to him, I feel as though he's getting tired but even in his own sickness, he was calling and checking on me every day, more worried about me than himself. Mama came to the hospital every day but we all thought it would be best if dad did not come even though he wanted to.

So, here I am, finally at home. Brandon helps me to my room, it feels good to be in my own bed and get some real rest. I don't care what anybody says, you cannot sleep or rest well in the hospital, they are always coming in poking, plucking, prodding, or something at all times of the day and night. I'm in lots of pain but I beg Brandon to go get me some real food because I'm hungry. "I could go for some orange chicken and 2 egg rolls," I said to Brandon, as I lean over to grab my purse. "I got you mama, you don't have to pay for it, Imma get me something too, do you want something to drink?" He says as he fluffs my pillows, taking care not to lean too closely. Yeah, I said, get me a sprite, a large one. Brandon leaves, promising to come right back so I grab my phone to check for messages and emails. I've got tons of messages, texts, inboxes, and calls but none from my own daughter today and none from Jeff since Brandon called and told him we were on our way home. I'm wondering what this so-called meeting he has at the church is about and why it's more important than me?

All of a sudden my phone beeps, there's a voicemail that I need to check. It's Brittany, she left a message saying she was just checking on me and that she's glad I'm going home. She promised to call and check on me later and said a quick, "Love you" and hung up. At least she checked in, I'm sure she was relieved to get my voicemail rather than speaking to me. I sure do wish we were closer than this but it is what it is and I take whatever love and attention I can get from her. I put the phone on the pillow next to me and slide more under my covers, I feel cold and in pain. I grab the remote to turn on my tv and before I know it, I'm in la la land, fast asleep.

I wake up to my phone ringing, as I grab it, I notice the time, it's after 3 pm, I slept for hours because Brandon and I got home a little bit after 11 am. I answer the phone and it's Jeff. "Hey, I've been calling you, why haven't you answered your phone?"

he screams. I slowly sit up and say, “Jeff I fell asleep and didn’t hear my phone ringing, I’m sorry” “Well, you heard it just now and picked up, I was worried about you”, he says with an ignorant tone. “Okay Jeff, I didn’t hear it at first but I’m okay, I just woke up”, I say softly because I don’t have the strength to argue. Did you try calling Brandon, he’s here. “What time are you coming home”, I asked. He proceeded to tell me that he will be home late because he has to go back to the office because the meeting at the church lasted longer than he thought. I asked him what the meeting was all about and he brushed me off by saying it was just a meeting with some people on the board of directors, some new people he wanted to put into place as trustees but before I could ask more questions, he asked if I needed anything and if Brandon was still around. He said he tried calling him too but he didn’t answer his phone either. I let him know that I was good and yes Brandon was here because I noticed the large sprite and fortune cookies on my nightstand, that let me know that he brought me food and probably didn’t want to wake me when he came back. After I hung up from Jeff, Brandon stepped from around the corner looking pissed. “I heard your conversation with dad mama, why is he tripping, calling you and fussing knowing you just got home from the hospital?” He said with an angry tone. “I put your food in the microwave because you were knocked out, you want me to warm it up?” I said, “yes but wait a minute Brandon, I don’t want you to get all upset with your dad, you know how he is, sometimes he doesn't know how to talk to people but he means well. He said he tried calling you but you didn’t answer” “Well, if he means so well then why isn’t he here?’ He shouts. “He should be home taking care of his wife, not me!” He screamed! “I’m sorry mama, I didn’t mean it like that, I’m not mad at you, I love seeing about you but you know I can’t stay much longer, I’ve got to get back home, I’ve got to go work and I’m scared that dad won’t be here for you like he should, who the hell does he think he is doing this? And no he didn’t call me, not that I know of”. Brandon’s face turns as red as a rose, I’ve never seen him this mad as though his anger is coming from a much deeper place than just this. “Brandon baby”, I say speaking softly, "your mad its seems, mama is gonna be alright, I'm not handicap honey, I will do what I gotta do, your dad will be here as much as he can I'm sure, don't worry about me, I'll be fine." I know Brandon didn't' believe a word I was saying because I didn't believe it either. He said, "Mama the doctors said it could take up to 6 maybe 8 weeks for you to be fully recovered, you can't go that long trying to take care of yourself especially since you still have to get chemo and radiation therapy. I think we need to call you a nurse to come out every day, just to help you shower and stuff you know, help take you to your appointments. Maybe I can ask Delores to come help me from time to time, I said to Brandon.

Delores was my best friend, my co-worker and she was a member of Grace Christian Center for years until she married for the third time and started going to "boring Baptist" with her husband, he was a deacon. Delores would be the perfect person but she lived too far from me and her husband James was super controlling, he probably wouldn't want her to do it. "Well, now that you mention it, Brandon, it probably would be a good idea but I don't know how your father would like it, he probably wouldn't want no one coming to the house, I said. Brandon said, well that's just too bad, unless he's gonna step up and see about you more, he has no choice. I'm gonna talk to him whenever he gets home because I leave in 2 days.

A few days later, after discussing things with Jeff and Brandon and doing a little research, we decided on a staffing agency that would be providing me a nurse. It just so happened that Brandon would be leaving to return home the day the nurse was coming. I was so nervous to be meeting this person, I was now having buyer's remorse, reluctant to have someone other than a close friend or family member waiting on me hand and foot, yet the damage was done, the nurse is scheduled to be here at 8 am this morning, this particular nurse came highly recommended by one of the staffers so the least I can do is brush my teeth and hair so I won't look too bad. Brandon comes peeking around the corner to see if I'm awake. "Mama you up?" he asked. Yea, I just need to get up and wash my face and stuff,

I know the nurse is on her way, I say softly. "I wonder what she looks like?" Bran chuckles as he helps me sit up and swing my feet on the floor. "I wonder if she's white," I said looking in the mirror at myself, I didn't recognize myself at all. I was darker, thinner and had bad circles under my eyes. I grabbed the Burberry scarf that lay on my dresser and wrapped it around my head as the first round of chemo and stress had started eating away at every hair follicle on my body. Brandon helped me get presentable as I now sit and wait for this nurse lady to show up. About an hour later, I could hear Brandon packing, zipping up his luggage then the doorbell rings. "I got it mom", he yells as he runs to get the door. My hands start sweating because I want to be a good patient but I know me, I'm a hard-headed know it all at times, most doctors and nurses make the worst patients and I don't want to run this lady away. Suddenly, I hear footsteps and whispers but I can't make out the voice. I just hope the nurse isn't a former co-worker, especially crooked teeth Hilda, she would always go around preaching that Catholicism is the true religion and she ain't even Catholic. The moment arrives, I sit up in my bed and look at what we have here, a male nurse. He's very handsome too. Hello, my name is Todd and I'm here to help you get well, he says as he extends his hand to shake mines. I kind of glance at his hands looking for a ring on his ring finger, why? I don't know but I adjust myself and put a smile on my face. "Nice to meet you, Todd, I'm Nadine and I'll try not to give you too much grief as I chuckle, kinda blushing a little bit because this man is very attractive. Tall, dark brown skin, light brown eyes, and curly black hair, he could be a model but he does have just a slight little belly, a good indication he may be in his early or mid-40's, you know how that goes.

So, after we go through my chart, medications, and doctor's orders, Brandon excuses himself from my room, grabbing his bags to take near the door downstairs. Mom, I have a plane to catch, maybe you should let dad know that Todd is here before I leave, he said very sarcastically. I don't know if he wasn't feeling Todd because he saw how I was looking at him or if he just didn't trust him since this was his 1st day on the job. So, I did just that,

I called Jeff and told him Todd was here, he sounded surprised that I had a male nurse but he didn't seem to care all that much. Jeff didn't seem too eager to meet Todd because by the time he would get home, Todd would always be gone. They had talked on the phone a few times but it would be 2 weeks before Jeff would put a face to the name because he actually took a day off one day to catch up on some things around the house but mostly because he had some bad sushi the day before that gave him the trots.

The morning that Jeff stayed home and worked, he was very attentive at first, making sure I could get to the bathroom and made a fresh pot of tea for me with some warm croissants but after a while, he was rushing to get me settled because he needed to get to his office downstairs. "What time does this Todd guy get here?' he said while looking at his phone. He should be here any minute now. He's late ain't he, Jeff said looking out the bedroom window. Yes but I asked him to stop at the drug store to get us some more crossword puzzles so it's okay. Us? Jeff said giving me the side-eye but before I could respond, we both heard the front door open. We had agreed to give Todd a temporary passkey so that I wouldn't have to go down the stairs to let him in but as he walked upstairs calling my name, Naddie, you up? Jeff's eyes bucked out like a man with thyroid disease when he saw Todd walk into the room, looking tall, smelling good, looking good even with scrubs on and he had a bouquet of fresh flowers in his hands. "For you my friend", Todd says as he hands me the flowers and a stack of crossword puzzles. "And you must be Mr. Broadnax, so glad to finally meet you face to face". He extends his hand but Jeff just stood there for a few seconds looking stunned, "oh, hey man, yes it's finally nice to meet you, you're a pretty tall brother, how tall are you and do you play basketball? They shake hands while Todd explains that he's 6"4 and never played basketball. Jeff then takes a sigh of relief, I know what he's thinking but I'll wait to see if he actually says it. So I abruptly interrupt by asking Todd to put the flowers in water in a vase in the kitchen then I grab the Carmex on the side of the bed and anoint my lips. Jeff is looking perplexed. Finally, after

Todd leaves to go to the kitchen, Jeff turns to me and snickers, so you got yourself a sugar booty huh? That's a term he used to call someone gay.

I said to him, Todd is not gay, he's been married but he's divorced. That don't mean nothing, maybe that's why he's divorced, he wants a man not a woman, he says sliding on his slippers laughing softly. I said, for your information, he's divorced because his ex-wife cheated on him. Wow! Said Jeff, as he turns and looks at me suspiciously, you sure do know this man's business, yall really been talking a lot huh? I said well, when you spend 5-6 hours a day with someone, you get to know them pretty well. I know you know and understand your co-workers, especially that paralegal intern, you really got to know her right?" Nadine, don't start that mess, you know I never messed with that girl, I couldn't help it if she had a crush on me. He hurried and grabbed his briefcase and headed towards the door, just call or text me if you need me, I'll be downstairs in my office. "It's okay Jeff, Todd is here, go ahead and do you, " I said, with a sinister smirk on my face, I was being plain hellish. I didn't have to say that, I know Jeff didn't have an affair, at least not with the intern but I still to this day believe he had one with his secretary, I can't prove it but it's just a feeling I got. I think that's why I have so much bitterness towards him.

The long nights at the office, the wine on his breath, and the perfume on his collar, it doesn't take a rocket scientist to figure out though Jeff has never confessed and I never had any other proof. I don't want to go down that road of thinking. Things are going well for me so far. I'm healing very well and Todd has been awesome. Not only is he a good nurse, but he's also becoming a good friend, driving me to my doctor's appointment for chemo, making sure I get up and walk every day. He even prepares or orders lunch every day. We have such a great time with the crossroad puzzles, catching up on all the Real Housewives series and even watching Good Times reruns when nothing else is on. He's becoming more like a companion than just a nurse. The scary thing is, I'm starting to feel something in the pit of my stomach whenever he comes around and when the weekend comes, I find myself missing him and thinking of him often. This is wrong, this is so wrong, I'm a married woman. I could never cheat on Jeff even though I'm sure he cheated on me. Why do I feel this way?

One time, after a chemo session, I was so sick, I was throwing up all over the place. I was too weak to wipe my own mouth, Todd grabbed a towel and wiped my mouth for me and cleaned up the vomit, threw up chunks and all. He then lay next to me in the bed and sang an old gospel hymn, the dude can actually sing. I remember just closing my eyes and humming along with him, it was at that moment he became more than a nurse, he was a friend, a special friend. That was the day our hands touched, but the moment that happened, Todd jumped out the bed and said he needed to chart while I took my nap. I believe he realized that day he crossed the line, maybe he felt something for me, deep in his heart. Maybe he got a whiff of my vomit breath and was ready to hit the door? We had spent countless hours together, looking through photo albums, preparing healthy meals, or at least he did, I just watched and he even took me to the barbershop for the big chop. All of my hair was coming out due to the chemo and radiation so I just decided to end the agony. Todd said I looked gorgeous but Jeff didn't like it but he said he understood because of my circumstance.

The walks in the park were special and we even started calling each other to gossip about the shows we watched together or anything that seemed important on the news. Jeff never knew about the phone calls but he would catch me smiling randomly and asked what I was thinking about. I always made something up, I could never tell him how I was fantasizing about Todd; how I was missing him like crazy on his days off, how I wish Jeff was Todd lying next to me in bed, and all the freaky things my mind wanted to do to him. I think Todd was starting to catch feelings towards me too. I hoped he did. I knew my thoughts of passion were totally against the vows I shared with Jeff. Somehow it felt so right even though I knew it was wrong. Todd was giving me everything I was missing from my own husband, love, attention, and his own way of showing affection without crossing the line.

We even became friends on social media so we could chat, it was less suspicious than phone calls. We'd share songs, recipes, and jokes. He told me that he went through all of my pictures on Facebook but didn't hit the like button because he didn't want my family to know we were friends. Every day he showed me just how much he cared for me, not just as a patient but as a woman. He was very attentive. He knew when I was having a bad day, he could tell when Jeff and I weren't getting along and on those days, he would try to cheer me up even more. He would also call or text Brandon for me and tell him my progress. Things started getting weird, Todd and I were acting more like husband and wife than nurse and patient. Even Brandon told me that he suspected Todd had a crush on me because he was way too nice, but I assured him that he was just doing his job. All along I was catching feelings for this guy and I felt so guilty. I was losing myself in this fantasy. I need to pull myself together, Jeff is literally downstairs in his office and I'm in here giggling with my nurse, this is crazy. I feel weak, not just in my body but in my spirit, I don't even recognize myself right now, I thought I would never feel this way about another man. Lord, I need your help.

Time goes on, the day is finally wrapping up and it's almost time for Todd to go home. Between the laughs, the talks, the nap I took and Jeff coming in and out of his office being nosey, I'd say it's been a pretty productive day. After Todd leaves, Jeff comes into the room with a very serious look on his face. "How much longer do you think you'll need a nurse?" he said as he peeked out the window to make sure Todd's car was gone. It seems like you're recovering very well now. I can't believe he's acting jealous, normally he acts like he doesn't care what I do, but before I could answer the doorbell rings. I thought maybe Todd forgot something but then he has a key, who could it be? Jeff goes to open the door as I stand at the top of the stairs, it's my mama. Normally she calls before coming, she's been to visit several times but it's been hard for her to come lately since dad hasn't been doing well but he refuses to get a nurse like I did. Jeff lets mama in, they start talking but I can barely hear them so I make my way out of my room to see what's going on. "Hey mom, I said as I slowly headed downstairs, how are you?" She walks to me and gives me a hug and just starts crying, she said, "your dad has been rushed to the hospital Naddie, I'm scared. I asked her why she wasn't there with him.

She told me that she ran to the store while he was sleeping, one of the housekeepers found him passed out in the bathroom and called 911, she was driving when she got the call. "I don't even know how I got over here, I'm too shaken to drive, Jeff can you drive me? He said of course as he rushed to get his shoes and sweater. I'm going too, I said, I need to know what's going on. I can feel my knees shaking and my palms sweating. Naddie, are you sure? You don't look well yourself. Mom, I'm fine, let me slip on some clothes, give me 5 minutes. I slide on my joggers and wrap a scarf on my head and get in the car with mama and Jeff, it's silent all the way to the hospital. "I think I need to call Rob and let him know too", I said while sitting in the back seat of the car. Mama always rode upfront no matter who was driving. I call Rob and tell him to meet us at Presbyterian Hospital where they took dad. I began to pray, I could see mama looking out the window with a tear rolling down her face. She looked scared and guilty, maybe she regrets going to the store at the time she did? Maybe she knew something we didn't know. I could see Jeff looking at me from time to time through his rearview mirror, I had no idea what's on his mind. All I could think about was my daddy right now.

Mama Rob said he'll meet us there, he was making a delivery in that area so he may get there before we do. Fifteen minutes later, we pulled up to the hospital, I felt something in the pit of my stomach. I was beginning to hate this place, having spent 25 years working here, being treated here for my own cancer, and the place where my parents have been coming for most of their adult life, I was really tired of seeing this hospital. My fondest memory was giving birth to my twins here, right now, everything else is just a blur. We get to the ER and I ask Carrie, a co-worker to lead us to where dad was. Carrie said, let me go get Dr. Henderson.

When she said that, my heart sank, I knew that Dr. Henderson was the EP, Emergency Physician, and protocol states that when a person dies in the ER, the EP has to notify the family. I couldn't speak, I didn't say a word because I didn't want to be wrong. I couldn't tell my mama that my dad was dead. I didn't want to believe it myself. I see Dr. Henderson walking towards us. "Who is this Naddie and why won't they tell us what room Robert is in? Dr. Henderson walks up to me and hugs me, "I'm so sorry Nadine, your father has passed away." Mama fainted and Jeff had to catch her. I thought I was gonna faint too but so many nurses gathered around, seeing about mama, getting her a wheelchair, asking me if I needed one. Total chaos had broken loose. I guess all nurses and staff wanted to do their best to comfort me and my family because they knew me. The Chaplain came from around the corner and RJ was with him, I guess he knew already, I could see the tears in his eyes.

He runs up to me and grabs me, hugging me real tight. He said, daddy's gone Naddie, he's gone, I was too late, I tried to get here on time; I was too late! He shouted and cried so hard it broke my heart. After the nurses wheeled mama in the grieving room, we all sat down to talk to Dr. Henderson. He said by the time dad got here he had already stopped breathing, it wasn't much they could do. I would be getting with his oncologist and primary care physician to get more info on his medical records and cause of death later, right now I needed to tend to my mother and my brother. RJ started calling family to tell them the sad news, he called his wife Shannon first but I asked him to let me be the one to call aunt Ruby, I knew she would take it hard and be even more over dramatic than normal.

Thirty minutes later, Shannon and the kids are at the hospital, dad's best friend Shane and his wife come up and I'm on the phone trying to keep aunt Ruby from coming. She wasn't in no condition to drive and I was worried about her blood pressure. She already had one stroke 2 years ago and I didn't want her anxiety level shooting through the roof. She is having a fit, dad was her only brother and they were super close. Maybe she should come? I don't know? I can't understand why anyone would want to come here, dad is dead and I myself am ready to go home.

My heart is beating out of my chest but I'm trying to remain calm. I haven't had a chance to cry yet, I mean I shed a few tears but I haven't really cried. I don't know who all Jeff called but I'm seeing some of the elders from the church arrive, they are comforting mama and RJ but I left the room, I can't take all this right now so I excused myself and found a wall in the hallway to lean on. It was getting hot in there and I'm starting to feel nauseated. Oh my God, I forgot to call the kids, I said to myself, I reach in my pocket to grab my phone then I see Jeff leave out the room, he's on his phone so I walk towards him, I heard him say I'm so sorry Brittany so I figured he was talking to our twin daughter. Is that Britt? I say while pulling on the bottom of his sweater. This red itchy sweater that I absolutely hate.

He turns and looks at me and nods, then he covers the phone with his hand and says, she's hysterical, I'm trying to calm her down. Well, I'll call Brandon then, I said as I walked back down the hall. I reached for my phone and before I knew it, I made a call I didn't intend on making. Hello, I hear this deep voice say, Hello Naddie, is everything alright? Chile, I done called Todd, oh my god. Hello Todd, I'm so sorry, I was trying to call my son and dialed you by mistake. It's okay, he said, are you okay? No, no I'm not, I'm at the hospital, my dad just passed away. Oh no, I'm so sorry baby, he said and my eyes looked like a deer in headlights because he called me baby. I was stunned, what did that mean? It was total silence for a few seconds. Hello, Naddie are you there? Oh, yea, I'm so sorry, I shouldn't have called you Todd, I'm just kinda out of it right now, I'm trying to be strong but I just wanna scream at the top of my lungs right now. I felt a tear roll down my face but I quickly wiped it away and shook myself back into a calm state. I didn't want to be seen crying, don't ask me why? I was always known to be a very stoic person but this is my dad for goodness sake, it's okay to cry right? Dad would probably tell me not to, he didn't like cry- babies.

Todd stayed on the phone with me, he comforted me and let me know he was there if I needed him. I began to hear commotion in the hallway so I rushed to get off the phone with him, for some reason I almost said I love you to Todd but I had to catch myself, I'm emotional, I needed to get back to my family, I needed to check on my mom. I pull myself together and walk back into the room where everybody was. Everyone was leaving, we needed to get back to mom's house and start making plans for dad's funeral but RJ said he thought it would be best if we did it the next day. I walked up to mom and kissed her, told her I loved her, and hugged her as tight as I could. Her body was weak, she was so exhausted, she said, Naddie go home, I don't need you getting sick on me, come to the house tomorrow morning you and Jeff, I'll be okay, Roxanne will be with me tonight. Roxanne was mama's housekeeper, she was old as the hills but she raised my mama and mama took good care of her. She really was like a mother figure to her, she lived in the guest house and was always around, she rarely did any cleaning, she just dusted from time to time. She was more like a companion for mama. Everyone was walking out the door yet I'm still looking for Jeff. I don't see him anywhere. I walked down the hall to where I had been previously standing and Jeff was there, stooped down on the floor, leaning up against the wall, I guess it finally got to him, he wasn't crying though but he did look disturbed. That conversation with Britt must have taken a lot out of him. Oh shoot! I said I forgot to call Brandon. So busy talking to Todd I didn't even call him, so I hurried up and dial his number, when he answered, I could tell he was crying. Mama, he said with a cry throat, I'm sorry to hear about paw paw, dad told me what happened, that man was my hero. I was just finna calling you, are you okay? I say as I'm looking around and seemingly guilty. I'm holding a baby, we're just now leaving the hospital. Some people came up here to pay respects to dad, they let us keep the body in the room for a while but they had to go ahead and get him to the morgue so the funeral home could pick him up. I'm just stunned, I mean we knew he was sick and the doctors did all they could do and dad was such a fighter, we didn't see this coming this soon. I'm walking down the hall towards Jeff as I'm talking to Brandon, I know he knows that I didn't call him, I hope he doesn't ask me why?

By the time Jeff and I get in the car, I'm already off the phone with Brandon, and its complete silence in the car. I just can't believe my dad is gone. I take a deep breath and Jeff says, how are holding up baby? The first thing I could think of is that he called me baby too. This is the second time today I've heard that term of endearment and I'm more surprised to hear Jeff say it than I was of Todd. I pull down the sun visor and look in the mirror, my eyes are swollen. Jesus, I look a mess, I said, as I tighten up the beautiful scarf on my head. Todd picked this one out one day while we were shopping together, I'll never forget that day, it was the day I stopped feeling ashamed of losing my hair because he had a way of making me feel beautiful with all that I was going through. I remember him saying, purple looks good on you, get this one. This beautiful silk scarf full of various shades of purple and lavender. Funny thing is, my dad loved the color purple too, the movie, and the shades. Girl, get yourself together, I say to myself in my head. Your dad just died and you can't stop fantasizing about this man. I close the mirror and stare out the window. You know that scarf on your head reminds me of a tie and handkerchief your dad wore one Sunday, Jeff said to me softly.

Was this dude reading my mind? I mean he just came out of nowhere with this one, I didn't even think he'd noticed. You know what, it sure does, I said awkwardly, I wonder if mama would like for us to dress him with his black suit and purple tie? Maybe, Jeff said, or maybe she'd want him in clergy attire? I guess we'll find out tomorrow when we go over there, I'm sure we're gonna have to pick up aunt Ruby cause she's in no condition to drive, she's taking this pretty hard. I know she would want to be there with us to plan the services. I'm so not ready for this. I can feel a tear trying to ease out of my eye. I quickly wipe it away before it can roll down my face. I'm trying too hard to be strong and I don't understand why? I guess it's because I need to feel strong no matter what. I feel tired and weak in my own body and now in my own head but that just wasn't who I, Nadine was.

Finally, Jeff and I get home and go to our neutral corners for a while. I head upstairs to the bedroom, get undressed and take this scarf off my head. I just stare in the mirror at myself for a minute, wondering what I did that made God so mad at me. Why was so much happening all at once? The bible says God won't put more on you than you can bear but I think my scales are off. I don't think I can take all of this and the scary thing about it is, my emotions are so jacked up, I can't truly express myself.

I really want to scream at the top of my lungs and knock all of this stuff off my countertops. Fancy perfume bottles, expensive lotions, Jeff's shaving cream, and special brush, none of this means anything right now. I pick up the scarf that I just took off my head and hold it close to me, clutching it for dear life. This scarf is bringing me so much comfort because it's in my dad's favorite color and it reminds me of Todd. I need a hug right now but Jeff is closed up in his office. He should be here with me, he should know how much I need him right now. He's acting strange but keeps checking on me throughout the night. Finally, around midnight, he gets in bed with me, I don't know what he's been doing in his office all this time. I thought I heard him talking but I'm too tired to care, I can barely sleep. Both the twins called again just to check in on me to make sure I was holding on okay.

They both will be here for the funeral. In the morning I needed to call and reschedule my chemo appointment, I already texted Todd to let him know that he didn't have to come for the rest of the week, he understood. He made sure to tell me that he would be here if I needed him and he asked me to text him and give him updates on how things were going. I found comfort in him caring but was reluctant to continue texting him, I'd rather see him in person but I know I have to wait. I've got a lot of busy days ahead, thank God the house is clean because I'm sure some family from out of town will want to stay here, it's no problem we have room and I don't want too many people at mama's house, getting on her nerves. My mind is on overload, it's about 12:30am and I still can't sleep. Jeff is knocked out. I slip downstairs to the kitchen, I pick up the phone and call my brother. RJ, are you sleep? Nah baby girl, I'm wide awake, I just can't believe dad is gone you know. I mean we knew it was gonna happen but I thought we'd all be by his bedside, he'd be in hospice or something, I thought maybe we'd be there to see him take his last breath.

I really thought we had more time. They said his heart just stopped beating, I just don't understand it Naddie. RJ began to cry again, I can't tell him to stop crying, I just didn't feel like crying right now, I don't know why. I missed my daddy too, I loved him so much! RJ and I talked for over an hour, we laughed, he cried and we laughed some more, just talking about daddy and how he raised us and some of the funny things he said. We both dreaded going to Mom's tomorrow, the reality of planning the funeral would certainly hit home. Suddenly, I hear footsteps creeping down the stairs, I'm like is that you dad? I said jokingly to myself but it's Jeff, lurking around the corner. Naddie, who are you talking to at this hour, he said with a slight attitude. I said it's RJ honey, neither one of us can sleep. Oh! it's RJ, he said with a sigh of relief. Who else did he think it was? Oh no!, did Jeff over hear my conversation with Todd at the hospital? Was that why he was looking dumbfounded when we were leaving, oh my god, I hope not. That's the last thing I need right now is more discord between us. I finally hang up from RJ and get back in the bed with Jeff. I snuggle up against him and spoon hug, wrapping my arms around his waist. Is this okay? I asked with caution. We rarely snuggled in bed together but I needed him tonight. Honestly, I needed to know if he knew I had been talking to Todd, I figured his response to my hug would tell it all but I still don't know. He grabbed my hand as I held him closer. I snuggled up against him even more as a tear ran down my face. Jeff turned over towards me and asked if I was okay. "No I'm not okay Jeff, my dad is gone and there is nothing I can do, I feel so helpless right now." He pulled me in a bit closer and kissed me once on my forehead then another kiss on the cheek and finally a kiss on my lips, passionately too. My heart was ready to burst, it had been a long time since we kissed like this.

I could feel his hands move across my body, I thought we would go to the next level but the kissing stopped. He ran his hand across my head, told me he loved me, and said I needed to get some rest. He then rolled back over and proceeded to place my hand back around his waist to continue with the spooning. I was stunned, I really wanted my husband to make love to me tonight but he didn't. Jeff hadn't touched me in months. What was all this sudden passion about and why did it suddenly stop? I was confused and I was hurt. I felt rejected and my stomach was in knots. I press my head a little closer to the center of his back. A sense of sadness overcame me once again. I felt my eyes water up once more and I almost had to cover my own mouth so as not to let out a scream of despair, instead, I closed my eyes real tight.

I finally was able to let another one out but what was this tear really about? Most likely it's a combination of my father's death, my own sickness, my own emotional hurts, or my guilt for wanting another man. I have to figure out how to get a grip, manage all these emotions like my daddy taught me, and put on a brave face. I must be strong for my family because I'm not comfortable with showing weakness. Can I pull it off, can I at least get through daddy's funeral without having a nervous breakdown? Only time will tell…

CHAPTER 7

THE FUNERAL

A week has passed and today is the day we bury my father. Once again, it's a rainy Saturday morning and as I sit in the bay window in my bedroom, all I could think of was my dad and Todd. I'm so pissed at Jeff right now I don't know what to do. Found out that Jeff permanently ended Todd's contract without talking to me first and I'm livid! Even though I am able to get around better on my own, I miss my friend, I miss his company and his secret affection towards me. I'm gonna fix that negro for this. "The cars are here", says Brittany as she yells upstairs to me and Jeff. Both Britt and Bran made it home for the funeral but no other family member wanted to stay at my house.

I'm kind of relieved that most of them from out of town decided to stay at one of the local hotels because it's already been a crazy week and I haven't been in the best mood since Jeff pulled his little stunt. The limos from the funeral home arrive, Jeff comes out of the bathroom adjusting his tie, I walk over to assist him, he smells so good, he's wearing the same cologne Todd used to wear. I dare not say anything about it, it seems the last few days he has been doing things to taunt me about Todd. I say to him with a smirk on my face, "you look very handsome Pastor". Thank you, he says as he strokes his hand through my hair, what's left of it. He looks at me in my eyes, staring at me like he has never done before. You're a strong woman Nadine, he says as he hugs me tight. I can see his face in the double mirrors behind him but he doesn't realize it. His words sound so sweet but the look on his face did not match the words, he looked sad but angry too. I'm pretty sure he suspects something went down between Todd and I.

That would explain the quick move to let him go. I hope he knows I didn't sleep with him even though I probably would've if the chance presented itself. I'm so ashamed of my feelings, after all, I'm a woman of God, a child of God for Pete's sake. How could I ever think about committing adultery? I've prayed many nights that God would take these feelings from me, I know I had to get control over my flesh. I had to repent for my emotional ties with Todd, a soul-tie is what it is. What we shared emotionally was not of God, I know that and I also know that my marriage needs work but so much has happened this year, I can't even think about how to resolve the issues Jeff and I have, not right now. I appreciate him though, he's being a trooper. He took control yesterday at daddy's wake and made sure people didn't' go overboard when paying their respects and giving speeches. We asked friends and family to speak for 3-5 minutes only and of course some folks wanted to act like complete fools but he didn't let that happen. He's been there for me, for my mom and for the church but I can tell he's hurting. I hurt him, Todd hurt him but there is something else weighing him down, I just don't know what it is; yet.

Me, Jeff and the kids pile into the limo, we head to mama's house where most of the family was gathering to do the procession to the church. There is complete silence in the limo, I can see tears rolling down both of the twins' faces. Brittany is holding her brother's hand and Jeff is holding mines. As we pull up to my parent's home, I can see cars all up and down the driveway and the street. Cars with different license plates, letting us know that people have come from far and wide to pay respects to my dad. Walking through the front door, I see friends and family I had not seen in years. I can't get through the crowd without stopping for a hello or a hug, all I want is to get to my mama. Brittany follows me to my mom's room, Roxanne is in here helping mama get dressed. I walk to give mom a hug and kiss, "are you ready mama?" I adjust her hat and look at her in her face. Her eyes are almost swollen shut, she's shaking like a leaf. Roxi walks up to her, handing her a beautiful white handkerchief, mama just looks at her, no words but half of a smile. "Yall go on now", said Roxi, God is with you. You're not coming to the funeral Rox? I said. No baby, I paid my respects to Rev yesterday at the wake, I'm gone stay here and tend to the house while yall are away, make sure these folks set up right for the repass. Okay then sweetie I said to her as I hugged her real tight, then she whispers in my ear. Take care of your mama chile, she ain't doing good... She pats me on my back and Brittany grabs mama's hand and walks out with her. I take a deep breath, headed to bury my dad, I still just can't believe it.

As all of the family load up in their cars, my legs begin to feel like strings of spaghetti. Thank God Jeff is holding me up because I can barely walk. I'm so concerned about mama, she looks like she can just throw up at any time, Lord help my mama get through this. Rob is looking pale and weak, he, Shannon, and the kids are riding in the limo with aunt Ruby while me, Jeff and the twins ride with mama. It's cloudy outside and last night's hard rain is now just a sprinkle, just enough to have the windshield wipers on and I can hear the squeaky sound of the limos wipers going back and forth, that's just how quiet it is in the car. For some strange reason, I turn my head and look back and see the long line of cars following us, all headlights on with a police escort. It made me feel proud of my dad. Pastor Robert Lee Payne Senior. A loving man who served God's people for over 45 years. He was noble, debonair, and funny.

I could hear his laugh right now, he always had jokes to tell, most of them were corny but I always laughed anyway. I wonder if my daddy made it to Heaven? Well, of course he did, he loved the Lord with all of his heart but sometimes I still wonder though. Dad had a mean streak at times. Plenty of times he would say something harsh or hurtful to mom that left her with tears. He always made it up to her by buying her expensive gifts, he never knew she gave a lot of those token gifts to me. She said she'd rather have his sincere apology and love than a mink coat or some earrings from Tiffany's. Why is my mind going there? I guess this is the beginning of going down memory lane? Man, this drive seems longer than usual, I whisper to Jeff. He gently squeezes my hand but doesn't respond. Mama is quiet, she clutches the handkerchief Roxi gave her then takes out her mirror. Well, we're here guys, straighten up, she says as she pats a little more powder on her face.

We turn the corner and a mass of family and friends are standing outside of the church, waiting for the first family to arrive. Everyone looks so nice, mama asked the family to wear black with a hint of purple. Of course purple being dad's favorite color and she wanted him buried in his purple clergy robe. As we pull up to the front of the church, the wind blows and the rain begins to come down just a bit harder. As we all get out of the car, Jeff grabs both me and mama to escort us both into the sanctuary but a strong wind blows mama's hat right off her head. Suddenly, a strange woman stoops down to pick her hat up and hands it to her. I've never seen this woman before, she looks young but I see that she needs help with fashion as I look her up and down. All I could see was a long black dress with red shoes and a red hat. She hands mama her hat without saying a word. Mama looks like she just saw a ghost. She softly tells the young woman thank you and we proceed inside the church.

Two hours have passed, so far the service has been beautiful, so many kind words spoken, some of dad's favorite songs have been sung and Pastor Dubois has given an excellent eulogy. Jeff is getting ready to wrap things up with his final words. Overall, nobody acted a fool, except a few church members who just wanted to be seen. Even aunt Ruby held herself up pretty well. Her boyfriend Fred met us here, he's been making sure she's okay and behaves. So many people are here, dad would be so proud to see all the love poured out for him today. I glance to my right and notice the sun peeking through the clouds, shining through the partially stained glass windows. I turn to the left and catch that strange woman with the red hat staring me down. Does she think she knows me? Is she a new member of the church or a long lost cousin that I have never met? She looks weird but I don't focus on her too long, we have to gather ourselves and get ready to head to the cemetery. As the family processions out, I caught Jeff eyeballing the red hat lady now I'm wondering who the hell she really is? Did this dude invite his mistress to my daddy's funeral? I'm gonna whoop his ass if he did. I can feel my blood pressure boiling but this is not the time to show my frustration.

We walk out together, headed to the limos, and low and behold, I see Todd walking out the side door. I can't believe he came to the funeral. Man! He looks good too, got shades on and a nice suit. Lord have mercy! I kept looking his way but he never turned around. I wonder if he saw me? I'm sure he did, he had to. Wow, he came and never even met my dad. I gather my composure and get focused on putting my dad in the ground. Dad would be so disappointed in me. I can hear him now, "Naddie, what in tarnation is your problem girl, you are a married woman. You may not be happy but you are still married, get it together before I knock you into kingdom come?" Whew, this little secret I have must stay between me and the Lord. I've been talking to Jesus about this because I don't want it, don't want these feelings, nor these desires. I take one more glance in Todd's direction but he's no longer there, I guess he went on to his car. I wonder if he's coming to the cemetery or repass? I doubt it. I've got to take some time to call and thank him for at least coming to the service. As we drive to the cemetery, there's a little more talking going on in the limo, I guess there is some relief of emotions since we got the service out the way but somehow I feel the worst is yet to come.

People tend to act a complete fool at the gravesite and even at the repass. I don't know why but they do. I'm so glad the rain stopped but the cemetery would still be a little muddy, that's why I'm so glad I decided to bring some slides, mama had hers too. We always took off our heels after church service because we knew we would be walking around greeting folks. Dad would always ask mama if she had her house shoes before leaving the house cause one time she forgot them and she made him drive all the way back home to get them. I chuckle out loud thinking about that time, I was a young girl then. What you laughing at mom? Brittany asks, I told her what I was thinking and before I knew it we were all laughing and talking about good times with dad but once we went through the big white gates of Gilead Park Cemetery, it got quiet again. We knew this would be the final stop to say goodbye to my beloved father.

As we gather around daddy's gravesite, I look out at the crowd of people, mostly family and long-time church members. I don't see Todd anywhere, I didn't think he would come but I do see that lady with the red hat. I'm perplexed because this chic came out of nowhere, I promise I've never seen her before. Now that I think about it, my own mama looked at her like she saw a ghost, I wonder if this is a woman who tried to push up on my dad or even worse, could it be that daddy had an affair? No way, not daddy. A lot of women in the church were in love with him but mama ain't no punk, she'd hurry and put those hussies in check. She even threatened daddy that she'd break his legs if she ever caught him fooling around. I find myself deep in thought as we sit in the chairs waiting for Pastor Dubois to say the final words, I can hear him talking but my mind has drifted to other things. I glance over at mama and her neck is as stiff as dad's dead body, she's gone emotionless. I feel a hand lay on my shoulder, it's my brother RJ, he and his family stand behind us because he let aunt Ruby and Fred have him and Shannon's seats. All the grandkids are standing together and I can hear the cries become more clear. Brandon breaks down and walks away, I want to go check on him but Jeff puts his hand on my thigh as to tell me not to move, Brandon will be okay.

Then I focus on Pastor Dubois, all I hear is, "ashes to ashes, dust to dust" as they begin to lower dad's body in the ground. Everyone in the crowd begins to weep then suddenly, the lady in the red hat runs to the casket and stretches her arms over the flowers that werewere laid on top, all I can hear was her scream, "my daddy's gone, my daddy's gone" she cried aloud. What the hell did she just say, I asked Jeff. I turn and look up at RJ, he walks towards the lady in a panic, saying, "who the hell are you, what did you say? Somebody better get this woman. Before he could reach her, Jeff hops up and grabs the woman by her arm, and pulls her away, some of the elders of the church were on post and helped him grab her. I heard Jeff say, don't do this Carla, this is not the time. I said, "Carla, who the hell is Carla and why is she saying my daddy is her dad? Mama, what is happening? Mama stands up slowly, looking stoic as ever, and says, meet me at the house. She didn't even flinch. She stopped crying and asked her church secretary to take her home. I'm following her towards the cars asking her what was going on and she never looked back. She said, "Meet me at the house Nadine" screaming at me as if I did something wrong. She looked totally embarrassed and pissed off.

She didn't even get to properly say her last goodbye because of this woman. I turned back to go back to the gravesite and some of the elders had escorted this Carla lady to her car and told her to leave. I can see Jeff and RJ arguing so I run to find out what was being said. RJ was livid, he asked Jeff who the heck was Carla and how did he know her. I can explain everything Jeff said but not here.

I go up to RJ and hug him, he hugs me back but still fusses about the situation then I just start to cry, I can't take this no more. People that had been at the site were still standing around being nosey so I burst out yelling for them to go home. "Go home, take y'all nosey asses home now" I scream. I cannot control my tears, Brandon walks up to me saying, "let's go mama, get in the car, I'm fighting with him saying no, I wanna talk to this Carla!. Jeff comes over and starts dragging me to the car, Brittany runs and grabs my purse off the cemetery chairs and follows us back to the limo. I can see Shannon and the kids getting back into their limo with aunt Ruby. Aunt Ruby is shaking and crying, I get back out of the car and go to them. Mama said for us to meet her at the repass at her house. Take me home, aunt Ruby screamed. Her eyes were bloodshot red. I don't wanna go to the repass, take me home. Aunt Ruby, you gotta be there, we need to find out what's going on, who that lady was, and why mama is acting crazy, she knows what's up and you are not going home. Aunt Ruby looks up at me with the eyes of Satan. I could see in her eyes that she meant business and that I had better leave her alone so I walk away and get back in the car. Jeff and the twins were going back and forth fussing and asking questions. I sit down and say "Everybody shut up, I don't wanna hear nobody speaking, the only person I need to hear talking is my mama and YOU Jeff". I stared at him with eyes that can burn a hole through the wall but I didn't want him to talk until we all got together.

We arrive at moms' house and I'm pissed. I can't believe that some of these greedy people have the audacity to show up to the repass just to eat knowing that our family has been turned upside down. Most of these folk were there when Carla pulled her stunt so they were just here to eat and be nosey. I walk in with an attitude, mama's cousin Mary walks up to me and says, "I told the family that they don't need to stay long and to give you all some space considering the circumstance so don't worry, I won't let anyone bother you. Your mama said to meet her in the Pastor's study. I give her the biggest hug and tell her thank you, I always loved cousin Mary, she was so sweet but she would get you told in a heartbeat so I'm sure she put the fear of God in family and friends and told them to hurry up, eat and get out this house. She was from Virginia and was staying as a guest at mom's house for the funeral.

RJ tells his kids to go get a plate and sit down somewhere, we were gonna meet mama in the study. I looked at my twins to say the same but Brittany said, "don't even try it mom, we ain't no kids, we need to know what's going on too." So I nod and tell them to come on. Me, Jeff, RJ, Shannon, and the twins are all sitting in dad's study. Roxanne peeks her head in and tells us that mama will be in in a few. She wouldn't let us in her room, anybody but Roxi which was absolutely ridiculous to me. As we wait I can see RJ looking at Jeff like he wants to kill him. All of a sudden, RJ says, hey man, how do you know this so-called woman, you said her name, how do you know her. Jeff looked so scared because all of us were wondering the same thing and staring at him like he stole something. This better be good, I said with an attitude. I want to know how YOU of all people know Ms. Carla with the red hat. Jeff just sat there, shaking, he said, let's just wait until Miss Diane comes in here. RJ hops up and grabs Jeff by the collar screaming, "nigga if my sister asks you a question you better damn well answer her.

The twins jump up to protect their dad then mama walks in. RJ turns him loose, she yelled, sit your ass down! WE all looked stunned, my mama rarely ever said a cuss word but she had fury in her eyes. She sat in dad's chair and said to all of us. "Now let me tell y'all something, I know y'all just lost your father and your grandfather but I lost my husband. Now I don't really feel like explaining myself or the situation right now but I will but first let me lay down the rules. Nobody and I mean nobody will interrupt me while I'm talking, ain't gonna be no bad-mouthing or fighting up in here either, she said while giving RJ the evil eye. I will talk then of course Jeff, you have something to say I know but then and only then, after we both say what we gotta say then can you ask questions.

We just sat there for a minute, waiting for her to speak. Brittany starts crying and Mama tells her to shut up and sit up straight. Mama then proceeds to tell us that many years ago, right before I graduated high school, daddy went to a convocation in New Orleans with some of the elders. He was gone a whole week but she found out that the Convocation only lasted two days and that he actually stayed in New Orleans for several days more after the convocation was over because he had met Carla's mother Caroline Boudreaux some weeks prior to that and had a brief affair with her. Over some time, Caroline became pregnant and started harassing dad for money. He eventually had to tell mama about her blackmailing him as she was threatening to expose dad's affair and his love child to the church. After a few years of paying her off they didn't hear from her for a while. Dad tried finding out where Caroline and Carla went, but no one knew so he just let it go. It wasn't until after me and Jeff got married that dad started getting letters from Caroline again and this time she was determined to expose the truth. So dad brought Jeff in on the scene as a lawyer to find out his rights and help him keep Carla and her mama away from the church and away from the family. This was all mama knew.

She explained to us that though she was deeply hurt by the affair, she was not willing to end her marriage and destroy all the hard work she had put into her family and the church. After mama explained her side of the story, she let Jeff speak and what he had to say was shocking to us all. Jeff explained that dad had confided in him about his affair with Caroline but the affair was not just a short-lived affair but he continued his affair for over 3-4 years with Caroline and that she and Carla had surprisingly come to the groundbreaking of the new church. He said after Caroline showed up unannounced, that's when he knew he had to end it.

He kept sending monthly payments for the child but that wasn't enough for Caroline because she became bitter and obsessed. She even threatened to come to the house to tell mama everything. Dad offered her $150,000 to leave him alone and she did after a while. She resurfaced a few times with threats and pictures but then dad had Jeff hired a private investigator to follow her. He found out that she had been operating as a psychic, duping people out of money down there in New Orleans. Dad was convinced she put a root on him and he threatened to have her arrested for extortion then expose her fraudulence and have her business shut down. She finally left him alone and it was years before the letters began to surface again. Dad told Jeff to rehire the P.I. and find out more stuff about Caroline, that's when they found out that Caroline had died in a car accident and that it was actually Carla who was sending the threatening letters. She had been coming to the church and meeting with Jeff and dad, she said she wanted people to know who she was. She wanted to expose her birthright as a child of the infamous Pastor Payne. She had pictures of dad with her mom, she had a shoebox full of letters that her mom wrote that dad had sent back. Jeff said a few times, he had caught her in the church trying to set up witchcraft and satanic rituals, he found a dead chicken in dad's personal office bathroom and some voodoo dolls on the premises of the church. Jeff said dad told him that he thinks Caroline did witchcraft on him and that's why he got lung cancer. He thought that she has some kind of connection with someone here in Cedar City because every time something big was happening in the church, Carla would show up. He thought for sure she knew someone who was a member or pretending to be a member of the church and that this person was keeping tabs on dad, giving Carla vital information. Dad had Jeff in charge of everything because Jeff knew what was going on and he wanted to make sure he kept everything a secret, especially from mama and the elders of the church. This explained the reason why dad made Jeff senior pastor. Jeff said he did not want to accept that position but dad made him. He wanted to protect his family from Carla's antics and he wanted to protect the church. Hearing all of this was so overwhelming, everyone in the study was stunned, crying, and filled with anger. My poor mom could not take anymore, she just laid on dad's chaise and curled under his blanket, and cried. She eventually told all of us to get out but I told her that I wasn't going anywhere. RJ stood up and flipped the end table and stormed out of the room, Shannon followed him out and I told the twins and Jeff to beat it, I needed my mama.

I shut the door behind me, slowly walking to my mom, I feel her spirit broken. I get down on my knees along- side of the chaise and she says softly to me, "I had a feeling he was still cheating, I had a feeling". She turns to me and lets out a cry that I never heard from her before. She said, Naddie, I can't take this, not only am I hurt that Rob is gone but I'm mad as hell at him, How could he do this to me?" I had no words, all I could do was hug my mama and let her get her cries out. So many emotions were going through me. I realized that the man I so loved and admired was a cheater, a hypocrite, and a liar. Dad had a long-time affair and had a daughter that I didn't know anything about and now she shows up here, what the heck? Why is she here? She probably wants money, insurance, or whatever. I stand up and tell mama I would be right back. She asks me to tell Roxi to come in there with her so I do that then go looking for Jeff. By this time, I can see only a few faces still here, cousin Mary ran most people off and wasn't letting anyone but family from out of town come in and eat.

I walk in the kitchen and Jeff and the twins are in there talking. I tell Jeff that I need to talk to him and to meet me upstairs in the first guest room. Jeff and I go inside the room and I try to gain my composure. I said, "Jeff, how could you have kept this from me, I'm so disappointed in you". I tell him that I always trusted him with everything but I felt betrayed by him and by my daddy. I could not express my anger enough, I told him that we must find out why Carla showed up to this funeral and what she really wanted. Jeff responds, "I'm so sorry this has happened, I had to keep my promise to your dad Nadine, I had to. Now just let me handle this situation with Carla, I don't want you to get involved in her schemes, this chick is crazy". "So you know her pretty well huh? I say sarcastically, I'm sure you do, well don't get it twisted, I will be there the next time you speak with crazy Carla, you think I'm gonna trust you to handle this alone? I can't trust you at all Jeff", I screamed. "Trust? Trust?" he yells as he grabs me at the shoulder. "I can't trust you miss innocent. You got your nerve talking about trust when you invite your damn boyfriend to the funeral, I'm surprised he's not here now." "What the heck are you talking about Jeff", I ask while pulling myself away from him. "What do you mean boyfriend?" Your little nurse friend, he says while getting all up in my face. "Yea, I know you been cheating on me with him, talking on the phone in the wee hours of the night, laughing and smiling all in his face, your ass been well, you just wanted that nigga around Nadine. "Now I see the fruit doesn't fall far from the tree does it, you just like your cheating ass daddy!" I slap Jeff in the face so hard it leaves a handprint. How dare you? I scream, "How dare you disrespect my dead father whose body aint even been in the ground for a day and don't you ever accuse me of cheating, I've never cheated on you, even though I had every right to. You never loved me, Jeff, you just tolerated me. You knew my family had money, you only stayed with me because of the twins. You weren't even there for me when I was sick and that's why Todd was there, it's your fault!" " My fault! Jeff screamed, you ungrateful b*@%&! All I have done for you, for this family and you tell me that I'm never there? I'm so tired of yall, tired of you playing the victim, tired of running behind your daddy, cleaning up his mess, keeping his mistresses quiet.

Do you think Caroline was the only one Nadine? Hell no, she wasn't, oh she was the only one he was dumb enough to get pregnant but not the only one he screwed around with". Shut up Jeff, you are a liar, shut up! I scream and run towards him, swing fists and try to bite him anywhere I can. We start tussling on the floor. "Get off me Nadine:! Jeff starts screaming, "get off me dammit!" Suddenly, Brandon bursts through the door. "What the hell?" He yells, get off her, get off my mama". He pulls me and Jeff apart and takes a swing at his own father. "Bran don't", I yell, as I grab his wrist, keeping him from knocking Jeff out. "I'm outta here", Jeff says as he hurries out the door. I sit down on the bed, I'm shaking like a leaf. Brandon sits down next to me, "mama what was that?" What the heck is going on around here? I'm crying so hard I can barely speak, I don't know son, all I know is my world has been torn apart, life as I've known it is over. This has been a nightmare. I lay my head on my son's shoulder and cry my eyes out. Brandon says nothing, I can just hear his heavy breathing. I'm scared he might hurt Jeff, I'm scared I might hurt Jeff. I've never felt so betrayed.

After a few minutes of sobbing, I go to the restroom to wash my face. I need to get myself together so I can check on my mama. Brandon and I go back into the study and Brittany and Roxi are in there with mama. I sit next to mom and ask her if she's okay. I've had better days chile, she says as she strokes my hair, how are you holding up? I've had better days too mama but I'll be alright, I'm tired though. Mama then tells me I need to go home because I didn't look good. I saw Brandon pull Brittany into the hallway while mama and I were talking, I'm sure he's telling her about the fight Jeff and I had. I stand up and ask Roxi if she's seen RJ. Well, ummm, he left, she said looking nervous. "He left, why?" I asked. He didn't say, I just saw him snatch them chillun' out the kitchen and said sumthin nother about leaving before he killed Jeff. Oh Lord, I better call him. I went to grab my phone but mama said, "leave him be Naddie, he's a man. Men process things differently. I suppose he's really mad at your daddy but just taking this out on Jeff". I suppose so, I say but I will call to check on him later. I asked mama if she wanted something to eat, she said "no just some tea". Roxi motions to go fix the tea but I tell her to stay with mama, I want to check on my kids anyway, I'll fix mama's tea. I walk into the living room but I don't see my twins, I call for Brit and she says, we're in the kitchen mama. I went into the kitchen and I could see the fright on her face and the fury on her brother's face. "How's grandma?" She asked. "She's calm, for now, have you seen your father?" "No!" Brandon yells "and he better not let me see him either". Brandon slams down the cup he had and crosses his arms. "I'm fixing mama some tea, yall wanna some?" "No, but I think I'm gonna stay here with grandma tonight if that's okay," Brittany says as she lays her hand on the small of my back. "Why Britt, you sure you wanna stay, Roxi is here, cousin Mary will still be here for 2 more days and I'm not leaving yet." "Yes mama, I just wanna sleep in the bed with my granny tonight, you know, just to make sure"… "Okay, then," I said, "what about you Bran, you staying too?" "Nah, I'm going home, I need to make sure YOU are okay." He said with an attitude. "I'll be fine son but it's up to you". Cousin Mary comes into the kitchen, she said she got rid of mostly everyone, some family even went to check into a hotel while others drove on back home. A few of the elders and their wives were still roaming around, putting up chairs, wrapping food, and helping clean the kitchen. She asked me if I had eaten and then gave me a plate wrapped in foil to take home. Well, I'm gonna check on your mama and head on up to bed she said, but before she could walk out the kitchen, mama came from around the corner. Her hair and make-up intact, she's greeting and telling everyone who was still there that she thanks them for the love and support and apologized for not coming out sooner. Everyone was understanding but you could see the curiosity in their eyes. They dare not ask what was going on, they just have mama her much-needed hugs, took their wrapped plates, and went on home.

Well, mama, Brittany says she wants to stay here with you tonight and cousin Mary is here but if you need me to stay I will, I say to her as I give her one more hug. No Naddie, you go and rest, I know you're tired and I don't need you relapsing on me, I'll be here, well, we will be here in the morning as she grabs Brittany's hand for dear life. I felt like she wanted me to stay but knew I had to get home to tend to my own husband. We say our goodnights and goodbye's, one of the elder Brown dropped me and Brandon off at the house, the lights are all off so I don't know if Jeff is here or not. I take a deep breath and head inside. I'm too tired for another fight, I need to feed Rollo and take a shower. I don't think he's here, Brandon says, as he starts turning lights on downstairs. Why don't you get some sleep son, I say to him as I kiss his forehead. I will, I'm gonna call Gina then head to bed. After I feed Rollo, he runs in the family room and sits under Brandon. Another one bites the dust I say as I chuckle, even Rollo has abandoned me tonight. I make my way upstairs, I'm feeling weak, realizing I have not eaten a thing. I go to my room and turn on the light, there Jeff is, sitting in the bay window in the dark. I'm a little scared, what has he been doing all this time, why is he sitting in the dark, and what is he gonna do next? Lord give me the words and the strength I need to get through this night.

CHAPTER 8

More Truth Revealed

After noticing Jeff sitting in the dark, I turn the lights on and proceed to gather my things to take a shower, I say nothing to Jeff because I don't know what to say. I decided to take a bath instead, I need to soak my pain away and talk to the Lord. I truly need Jesus now more than ever. I run my bathwater, as I go back and forth from my room to the bathroom, Jeff still sits silently in the bay window, never looking at me or talking to me. I decided it's best to remain quiet, I'm too weak and exhausted for another fight. Once I get in the tub and slide down to soak my entire body, Jeff walks in. Nadine, we need to talk, he says. Well, talk Jeff, I'm listening, I speak softly as I run the bath sponge up and down my legs. Jeff begins his speech, Well, first, I want to apologize for everything, I mean everything Nadine, I'm so sorry your dad is gone, I loved Pastor Rod, I really did, he was like a father to me, secondly, I'm sorry that I loved and honored him so much, it made me dishonor you as my wife, I'm sorry I kept his secrets from you and the whole family, I'm sorry about Carla being here and all the truth that had to come out on this day, I'm sorry for causing so much pain. I see a tear roll down his face and then he gets on his knees and grabs my hand, he kisses my hand and asks if I would forgive him.

Of course I forgive you Jeff, I mean, I have to forgive you if I'm gonna please God but I must admit I'm very angry, not just at you but at my dad, at Carla even my mama. Your mama? Jeff says looking perplexed. Yes, I'm a little mad at her too, she knew about some of this stuff and never told me anything, I guess most of my pain comes from not knowing and not being able to hear my dad speak for himself. Suddenly, I began to cry, cry so loud and so hard that I couldn't contain myself. Jeff grabs me and holds me, he then helps me out of the tub, puts on my gown, and lays me in bed. I feel so weak, I feel sick. Have you eaten anything today Nadine? He asks. No, I haven't, cousin Mary fixed me a plate, maybe I should eat some of that because I need to take my meds, I feel a little anxious. Jeff goes downstairs to warm up the plate I had from the repass, meanwhile, Brandon comes upstairs to tell me he's finally going to bed and asks if I needed anything before he lays down. No, your father is warming up my food from mama's house, you get some sleep I say as he hugs and kisses me goodnight.

Have you spoken to your father Bran? I asked before he walked slowly out of my room. NO! He shouted I don't have anything to say to him right now mama. I have never heard such a tone come from him like that before, he sounded like he hated his own father, I truly hope it's not because of me. We both hear Jeff's footsteps coming from downstairs. Goodnight mama, I love you said Brandon as he exists before his father makes his way to our room. Jeff hands me my plate and a glass of ice water. Nadine, he says softly, I know me, you and the twins need to have a conversation about what went down but we can do that tomorrow, I know Brandon is pissed at me right now and Brittany texted me and said she was staying at your mom's house tonight, so this gives us all a chance to cool down and talk rationally tomorrow. I agree, I said, I'm just too tired right now, my emotions are all over the place. I unwrap my plate and see all this food piled on, I know I'm not gonna even eat half of this but I do want some of this chicken and macaroni and cheese. I noticed Jeff had made his way back to the bay window, he just keeps staring out the window as if someone is talking to him. Jeff, Jeff,

I say aloud. He turns quickly as if I startled him, he must have been in really deep thought. I asked him if he could please give me a little more barbecue sauce for my chicken, it must have gotten a little dry when he warmed it up in the microwave. He takes my whole plate with him back downstairs and I wait. Meanwhile, I hear my phone chime, someone sent a text message. I grab my phone and it's a message from Todd.

Oh my God, why is he texting me now? I read his message: Nadine, I want to send my condolences to you and your family again, I'm so sorry for your loss. I know you loved and adored your father and my heart hurts for you. I saw you at the funeral, I came to show my support for you, you looked beautiful. I just want you to know that I will miss you but it's okay, I already have another patient, just know that no one will ever take your place, love Todd. Wow! I don't know how to feel about this text right now, part of me is happy to know that he did care for me, more than a patient, more than a friend. The other part of me is feeling guilty as hell, how can I be mad at my dad for cheating when I am walking on that same path. I never slept with Todd but that doesn't matter, I crossed the line with my feelings, I started to like him in a way that a woman likes a man she wants to be with.

Even though I'm torn emotionally and feeling convicted spiritually, I couldn't help but notice the smile on my face while reading this text. I'm not gonna respond, I say to myself, I can't, I shouldn't, I won't. Then I hear Jeff coming back so I throw my phone under my pillow and sit up straight. Jeff walks in but he has this sinister look on his face, he hands me my plate and when I look down at it, I'm stunned. Jeff had poured barbeque sauce all over my plate, not just the chicken but everything. I say, Jeff why did you do this? I immediately started crying, this was just cruel. Jeff, why did you do this? I asked again as I stared up at him with tears in my eyes. He said it's been years since I've seen you smile at me the way you were just smiling at that text. Was that your man texting you? Was that Todd? He says as he starts moving the covers around searching for my phone. Stop it, Jeff, what are you doing, Stop it! I screamed! The plate falls off my lap onto the floor, I'm tussling with Jeff as he pulls my phone from under my pillow. He grabs the phone, goes through my texts and reads every word Todd sent me. I'm begging him to stop it, I get out of the bed trying to get my phone out of his hands and suddenly, he throws my phone up against the wall and breaks it, he starts yelling at me, asking me why I cheated on him, why Todd?

All of a sudden, Brandon comes in and knocks his own father dead in his mouth. He hit him so hard that Jeff fell down. Brandon is standing over him begging him to get up so he could do it again. Jeff is so stunned he can't move. I've been waiting over 15 years to do this, he screamed! Brandon stop it, what are you talking about, stop this! I go to grab Brandon but he snatches away from me. No mama, I'm sorry but you need to hear this too. Remember this dad? Taking me and Brit for rides to your girlfriend's house? Remember telling me not to tell mama and giving us money, buying us ice cream and stuff like that was supposed to make it alright. We were around 10 years old when it started, you would be at work mom and I guess he knew he couldn't leave us at home alone so he started taking us with him, to the office, to restaurants, and to their houses. At first, he told us that these women and her children were our cousins but then when I started asking too many questions when I got older, he stopped taking me. You wanna know why Brittany can hardly stand you mama? It's because of him, he always told her negative things about you, he told her that you were mean to him and that you didn't love him no more. She told me that he said he never wanted to get married but that you trapped him when you got pregnant. He convinced her that you were the reason why he had these "little lady friends". He made sure they were nice to her too, all the extra money and gifts, they came from his girlfriends. I wouldn't let him bribe me that's why we stopped being cool, and Brittney selfish ass, she liked the money, the designer clothes and handbags so she kept his little secret for her own benefit, it's her guilt that causes her not to get along with you mama, you didn't do nothing to her, nothing to him either. Man, I hate you! He screamed at Jeff! I'm outta here! He leaves the room, grabs his phone and keys to my car and leaves.

Jeff gets up, his mouth is bleeding, tears rolling down his face. He goes into the closet and grabs a suitcase, he starts packing some clothes. I'm sitting on the bed in total shock. I asked Jeff where he was going? I'm going to a hotel Nadine, I'm not finna sit in this house where you let your son disrespect me like that. I need to get away from here, away from all of yall… He grabs his bag and leaves. I'm sitting on my bed crying my eyes out. Food all over the floor, my comforter and sheets ruined with barbeque sauce and my cell phone is destroyed. I'm in a blank stare, I can't move. I cannot believe this day, the day all hell broke loose for me, for my family. Lord Jesus, where are you? I need you, I feel hurt and alone. I'm shaking like a leaf. I begin to clean up this mess, Rollo finally comes upstairs and hops in my bed, he looks petrified. All I could think is that the cancer didn't kill me but my family will. This is way too much for me. I don't even bother to change my linen, I just curl up in a ball and cry myself to sleep.

It's the next morning, I feel someone shaking me out of my sleep. It's Brandon, telling me it's time to get up. I look up at him, he still has a rage in his eyes. I ask him what time is it? It's a little after 10am he says as he starts cleaning up the mess we left behind last night. I didn't see dad's car when I came back home this morning, did he leave last night, he asked. Yes, he packed a bag and said he was going to a hotel, he broke my phone so I just… Brandon interrupts me and says; you don't' have to explain yourself mama, you've been through so much, I can't imagine how you feel. He proceeded to tell me that my mama called and asked what time we were coming over today because she wanted to talk with me and RJ. I need to call my brother, can I use your phone Bran? Of course, mama, he said as he pulls his phone out of his back pocket. Why don't you go in the bathroom and get ready and I'll clean up this mess.

I do as he says and go into the bathroom, sitting on the edge of my large garden size tub. I think back for a minute when Jeff and I bought this house, how we used to take baths together all the time, the twins were little so once we put them down for the night, it was all about us, the love and romance was so real then.

His hands felt so strong as he stroked my hair and washed my back. I loved everything about him, his smile, his hair, his lips so soft and kisses so warm, who would have ever thought we would end up like this. I shake myself back to reality and call RJ. I told him mama wanted to meet with us this morning but I felt the need to meet with my brother one on one so I suggested he and I meet at the church around 2pm, he agreed. This way, the church would be empty because everyone from 8am service would be good and gone. After I showered and got dressed, Brandon made me eat a little breakfast then he proceeded to mama's house, grabbing his sister's overnight bag so she could change clothes over there. I took my time getting dressed as I was feeling a lot of pain and weakness in my body. I also wanted to get my emotions under control and take time to think things through before RJ and I met with mama. I proceeded to drive listening to smooth jazz radio in the attempt to get some relief from my emotional pain. As I pull up to the church, I see RJ sitting in his SUV waiting for me in the parking lot.

I get out and walk to his car. Why are you waiting out here, you could've sat inside and waited, I said as I approached him. He gets out of the SUV and grabs me, hugging me so tight. We notice the signs out front that says in honor of our beloved Pastor Payne and his family, we will only have 8 o'clock service here at the church but please visit the website for our online service Sunday morning at 10am. The elders and associate pastors came in and recorded a short service along with the praise team. Mama thought it best we do it that way so we wouldn't be harassed today by spectators and nosey roseys. The decision was made to do this while we were planning dad's funeral. I'm so glad we did because it would have been a hot mess having to show up here on today. So, we walked into the sanctuary together, there were still some flower arrangements from the funeral around the pulpit, there was still an eerie feeling hovering in the sanctuary. Do you wanna sit in here or go into my office? I ask RJ. I'm fine in here he says as he takes a seat in the middle aisle, not too far back but not right upfront either. RJ puts his head down for a second then he just starts opening his heart to me. Nadine, first let me apologize to you, I'm sorry that I just up and left you alone to deal with the whole fiasco at mama's yesterday.

I had to get out of there before I hurt someone and Jeff was at the top of the list. I'm mad as hell at him right now but I'm also mad at dad, how could he have done all this? As I look up at that pulpit, the podium he stood behind for over 2 decades, everything seems like such a lie. And mama, smooth and sophisticated Lady Diane Payne, she just sat here with that phony smile, she knew about his affair or should I say affairs. I mean I would hear things like dad was a flirt and I knew a lot of women in the church were after him but I never imagined him doing what he did. And now this Carla chic coming on the scene, literally ruining my daddy's home going with her antics and embarrassing the family like that, I just couldn't take no more. I'm so sorry Nadine, as your big brother, I should have at least stayed for you. I mean you're going through your own personal battle with your health, your marriage and God knows what else, I feel like I let you down and I'm so sorry. I grab my brother's hand and tell him it's okay. RJ, this is not just about me, you're having to endure all of this too. I'm sure it's taking a toll on you as well.

I can't expect for you to lay your feelings aside to see about me, we just have to be there for one another and I'm here for you brother, I love you. RJ and I sat in the sanctuary crying and talking for more than an hour. We had to figure out how we were going to move forward, what we were to do about this Carla situation and how we could support our mom. We were just about to gather our things and head out to mama's when we heard some rambling around in the hallway. We both leave the sanctuary, going towards the offices when we see Jeff with bags and boxes stacked up outside dad's office. Jeff what the heck are you doing? I yell. Yea, what are you doing with our daddy's stuff? RJ says and he runs towards him like a running back in the NFL. RJ, please don't hit him, I scream. Too late, RJ pushes Jeff down so hard, he knocked everything out of his hands. This time, Jeff hops back up quickly, I guess he's tired of getting his butt beat and he attempts to put up a fight. I quickly jump in the middle of my brother and husband and beg them not to try and kill each other. RJ starts to pick up the files Jeff dropped. Man, what you doing with all this, you stealing church files now? Man get out of here, you ain't the pastor no more, I'm gonna make sure of that, he says as he looks at Jeff eye to eye with no fear. You can't fire me RJ, I quit! Jeff yells, and even if I didn't quit, you don't have authority to put nobody out of this church, you barely even came. You let your idiot white wife keep you from supporting your own daddy, she had you going to some cult church with her, that's why your daddy relied on me, cause he couldn't rely on you! I guess that felt good for Jeff to say that but I'm sure it wasn't worth the butt whooping he got afterwards because RJ dropped every file in his hands and went to whooping Jeff's behind like he stole something, literally.

It took me a while to pull my brother off of him, he beat him pretty bad but Jeff deserved it, he crossed the line once again and I couldn't save him this time. Jeff once again started picking up files off the floor, telling us that though he may not be the Pastor of the church anymore, he is still dad's legal representative and he had the right to confiscate the files. Everything else was his own property so we let him take his stuff, RJ made sure he got the set of keys from him and kicked him out of the church. I just stood there, I had no words, I was hurting too bad to show I cared but deep inside I did. After all this, I still loved him, I mean I didn't like him at the moment but I loved him, still. So, RJ and I cleaned up the place, we went through dad's office a little bit, reminiscing on the good old days for a moment. I grab his calendar book, an old flip phone and his bottle of anointing oil and we walk back into the sanctuary, headed out the front door to go over to Mama's. I'm sure she was worried about where we were. Suddenly, I had an urge to stay back. It felt like something literally pulled me back, keeping me from going out the door.

I knew it had to be the Holy Spirit. I've had these encounters before, mostly in the middle of the night when the Holy Spirit would wake me up. I knew in my own spirit that this had to be God. I told RJ to go ahead because I needed to take some time and spend with the Lord. He asked if I was sure, he seemed to be worried just in case Jeff came back but I reassured him that I was being led by the Holy Spirit. I left and I locked the doors and went back into the sanctuary. I went to the altar and got on my knees and started to pray: Dear Lord, first I want to thank you for being God, the creator of heaven and earth, all the glory and honor belongs to you in the name of Jesus. Father, I come as humble as I know how, I come to you because I need you Lord, yet, I feel so far away from you right now. I'm sorry that I let you down Lord, I'm sorry that I have caused so much pain.

I'm sorry that I have not been who you called me to be. Father, now that dad is gone, so much has happened, the truth has been exposed and I need your strength and guidance to help me get through this. Lord, I know that you see and know all things, there is nothing hidden from you. You've seen me fall in love with another man that is not my husband, you've seen my heart and the resentment I had toward my own husband and even my own daughter. You knew what my dad was doing, you knew what my mother was allowing. There are so many secrets revealed and maybe some still yet to be revealed, nevertheless, I come repenting and asking for your forgiveness in Jesus name. God, I don't know how to proceed so I'm yielding under your power and authority. Please take care of my family, my mama, my brother, my children and even my husband. Teach me how to forgive, give me the wisdom on how to lead my family during these trying times. Give me insight on how to handle Carla and reveal to me her motives if there be any and Lord, make your spirit known to me now, help me, equip me and freshly anoint me for the journey and tough road ahead in Jesus name I pray, Amen.

As I closed the prayer, I felt a peace rest upon me, I hadn't felt this peace in a very long time. I knew in my heart that God heard my prayers and answered me. Tears rolled down my face as I worshipped and praised God for his grace, mercy and everlasting love. I looked down and noticed a distinct purple rose petal laying on the 1st step of the pulpit. I took it as confirmation from my dad that I had to spend this time in the presence of the Lord. I then began to hear the voice of the Lord instruct me on what to do next. The fear of the Lord gripped me, I knew I had to obey. I was apprehensive at first but the Holy Spirit gave me peace. I knew I had to head to mama's house with authority. God wanted to clean this mess up and he was gonna use me to do it but first, I had to allow him to clean my own personal mess up. Lord I'm gonna need your wisdom, I said as I got in my car. I knew God was speaking to me, all I could do is listen and allow him to order my steps.

I pull up in front of my parent's home, the Lord has been talking to me all the way here. I'm still crying my eyes out, for so many reasons. I'm worried about Jeff, I'm worried about the twins, my brother even my aunt Ruby, I haven't heard from her, she never showed up to the repass. In fact, I decided to call her. I had gotten the church emergency cell phone from dad's desk because I didn't want to be driving around without a phone. I called aunt Ruby and she sounded reluctant to speak to me and she told me that mama had invited her to come over too but she didn't want to go. She told me that she was shaken up by the whole Carla thing because dad told her about his affair and love child and that she and my mama had this whole discussion about her not letting some witch take her family from her. She was so apologetic but I felt like there was so much more that she had to say. She said that even though she really didn't really want to come over but mama insisted that she come because there were some things she wanted to discuss about dad's will. I told her that I was sitting in front of the house and would wait for her to arrive since she mentioned that she was already on her way.

I just sat there waiting, watching the gardener water mama's flowers and mow the lawn, all the staff were busy going on throughout the day as if nothing had happened. I mean we literally just buried my father yesterday and no one seems to care anymore. Perhaps they want to grieve but mama won't let them. The only one who seems to give a darn is Roxi, but of course, Roxi has been on the seen since I was a little girl, hell since my mama was a little girl. Mama treated Roxi like she was her own mama, better than my grandma even because mama don't even talk that much about her. Mama has given Roxi so much, she's given her family money, a home and expensive gifts. Years ago when she had a stroke, Roxi's own kids tried to hurry up and put her in a nursing home but mama wouldn't let them. They did end up finding a way to sell her house, claiming she was incompetent and they took her money, that's when mama let her move in with her and dad. Mama does more for Roxi now than Roxi does for her. She just keeps her on staff to make sure she's good because all she does is make tea and do a little dusting. Anyway, I see aunt Ruby pull up, her boyfriend Fred lets her out the car but he doesn't get out. I walk over and speak, I say, Fred aren't you coming in? He says, Nah, I'm just gonna sit out here and smoke my cigarette and wait, I'm listening to the sports station so I'll be alright.

I lean over into the car window and give him a hug. I walk around to meet aunt Ruby, how you doing sugar? She says as she grabs and hugs me so tight. I'm okay but this is a lot auntie, I say as I kiss her on the cheek. I kind of chuckle because she smells like cigarettes and sausage. "Well, let's see what my brother has to say, he always wants the final words, just like at church, he has to say the benediction", she says sarcastically. We both laugh and hold hands as we walk up to the grand front door of the Robert and Diane Payne compound.

We just don't know what in store for us. I can see that RJ and Brandon are already here. Mr. James waves at us as he trims the hedges but he's looking crazy like he knows all hell finna break loose. The birds are chirping and the sun is shining but somehow I feel a dark cloud is over this house. My knees are starting to shake because I have no idea what's in my dad's will, is that even why mama wants us to come over? I know we have to finish the discussion that went wrong on last night but deep in the pit of my stomach, I feel another storm brewing and the name of this Hurricane is Carla.

CHAPTER 9

A New Journey Begins

Aunt Ruby and I walk in the house, it's such an eerie feeling to know that my dad is gone. Normally he would be sitting in the family room, reading the newspaper or working on his laptop. I'd walk over and say, "What's going on old man?" and He'd look up at me with those big brown eyes and say, "I got your old man sassafras". I chuckle as I think back on those times, everything is still so fresh. I look around and there are so many flowers in the house, flowers from the funeral, from families and churches who sent their condolences, it's a beautiful mess. "Mama, where yall at?" I yell as aunt Ruby and I head towards the kitchen. We're in the dining room mama, Brittany says as I hear her smacking on some food. We walk in the dining room and everyone is sitting at the table chomping down on brunch that mama's cook and Roxi made this morning. I go over and give mama a kiss, she looks a little dazed but still holding it together. I looked down at her plate and noticed she hadn't touched any of her food yet, I'm not surprised, She never eats when she is stressed. She already lost around 10 pounds dealing with dad's sickness this past month, she's gonna be thin as a rail in a minute. I chose not to address it and move on the hug and kiss my nieces and nephew, my own kids then RJ and Shannon.

Aunt Ruby follows suit then makes her way to sit in the empty seat right next to mama.

I see aunt Ruby grab her hand and softly speak something to her, I suppose she is just encouraging her and letting her know she is there for her. I grab some fruit, a cup of tea and croissant and sit next to my kids. There's a lot of small talk going on and I notice that Roxi keeps making her way back and forth from the kitchen to the dining room just to check on mama. RJ makes eye contact with me and looks at me as if he wants me to be the one to start the conversation on why we all are here. I shake my head saying NO! He doesn't know that I don't have the strength today, usually I'm the strong and aggressive one but he needs to take charge today. It's so funny because we both are arguing with our eyes as if to say, "you do it, no you do it". We go back and forth for a minute then finally RJ says, "so mama, when are we gonna have this conversation?" I mean, I'm not trying to rush you or anything but… there was dead silence for about ten seconds then she says, I'm waiting on Jeff to get here then we'll talk. Oh Jeff is coming? He says as he throws his fork down on the plate and leans back in his chair disgusted.

I can hear Shannon whisper to him, Rob don't start, stay calm. She grabs his hand and rubs it, knowing she has to do something to soothe the savage beast. I look at RJ and remind him that Jeff is still dad's executor and he is the one who is reading the will. I'm staying calm myself because I know God has sent me here with another purpose, I still feel the peace that rested upon me while I was at the altar this morning. Then mom begins to say something that almost shook me to the core. She calmly said to us, everyone in the room. "Jeff is not coming alone, I asked him to bring Carla with him." What! Aunt Ruby yells, out, why on earth would you have that demon child in this house Diane?" Mama began to sit up straight and it seemed as though she was looking at all of us in the eye at the same time. She seemed strong again as if she had to force herself to take charge and her voice was very commanding. "I told Jeff to bring her for the reading of Rob's will, I know he left her something and she has the right to know what it is and then I hope she gets whatever it is she is to inherit then get out of our lives forever". As soon as she said that, the doorbell rings, I could hear cousin Mary go to the door and greet whoever it is, knowing in my heart that it is Jeff and Carla.

I take a deep breath and look at RJ, motioning him to stay calm. Brandon puts his hand on my back and asks if I'm okay, I say yes and take another deep breath. Cousin Mary escorts Jeff and Carla into the dining room. Carla looks nervous, (rightfully so) and Jeff is looking like he could pass out at any time. Hello everybody, Jeff says, I'd like to introduce Carla to yall. She said, Hi everyone, it's so nice to finally meet you all. I'm so sorry we had to meet under these circumstances. We all say hello but with very little enthusiasm then Mama asks them to come in and have a seat, she offers brunch but the both decline. "Well, if no one else is going to eat then perhaps we should all go into Rob's study", mama said as she stood up and gently places her lap napkin on her 'untouched plate. RJ tells his kids to go watch tv but mama said, "no, everyone needs to be in the room". So we all get up and head to dad's study. I nudge aunt Ruby and tell her that I really wanted to address the family before the reading of dad's will but I suddenly got scared. "What you gon say chile?", she asks as she pulls down her skirt and appear to adjust her girdle underneath. "Don't be starting no mess Nadine she said giving me the evil eye, it's enough going on as it is with your mama bringing that hussy up in here". "It's not like that" I tell her as we proceed to walk down the hall, it's something positive that the Lord is leading me to do, I said with a tremble in my voice. Well, if the Lord told you to do it you best be doing it then, she said as she walked past me, hurrying to find a comfortable seat in dad's study. I was the last one to walk in. I see mama standing behind dad's chair at his desk. I can't believe how stoic this lady is. Her eyes may be a bit puffy but her neck is stiff as stone. "Everyone, find a seat, children, you may sit on the floor, she says as she extends her hand as if she is in some sort of beauty pageant. She opens her mouth to say something but I politely interrupt her and say, "Mama, if I may, I have something I would like to share. I went to the church this morning and prayed and the Lord spoke to me and told me to do something and I must be obedient, I have to do it before Jeff reads the will".

She looks me square in my face like she is saying in her head, ``How dare this child interrupt me but she humbly responds, "By all means, Naddie", she takes a seat in dad's chair and continues to stare at me. I can hear her voice in my head, "this better be good Naddie". So, I walk to the window, knees trembling and all but ready to speak what's on my heart. "Last night I had a dream, I dreamt that I was reciting Dr. Martin Luther King's I had a Dream Speech, not in front of a mass of people but only in front of all of you. Oh Lord, I heard Brittany say softly under her voice. I stop for a second and look at everyone, I could see mama looking at me as if she's saying hurry up, RJ's kids are on the floor, Lindsey is drawing circles with her finger on the soft Persian rug, Chad is digging in his nose as usual and Jessica is actually looking at me, paying close attention to what I'm getting ready to say. Brandon and Brittany are looking anxious, I'm sure they want to get straight to the reading of the will and RJ and Shannon look confused because they don't know where I'm going with this, Aunt Ruby is staring at Carla like she wants to chop her head off and Carla isn't making eye contact with nobody, she's sitting in the corner, away from everyone, I can tell she is super uncomfortable and probably wants me to hurry up so she can get her goods and get out of here. Jeff looks worried and stressed, I can tell his hands are sweating because he keeps wiping them on his pants. Everybody is looking at me, staring, wanting me to continue my story, so I complete my brief scan of the room and proceed with my message. "Dr. Martin Luther King was a great man, God chose him to lead our people to the promised land of our civil and human rights. Not just talking about heaven but the promised land of this nation, to have freedom and liberty which is supposed to be all of mankind. He had his trials and tribulations but he continued to pursue the reality of his dream, yet, in all of his good deeds and the call God put on his life, he wasn't perfect.

It is said the Dr. King cheated on his wife, allegedly and accused of infidelity, he smoked and sometimes cussed. I don't know if any of those rumors are true but did that change who he was as a man in totality? No, he still was able to accomplish so many great things in his life, many that we are privileged to experience right now, so in essence, his dream is fulfilled. I say that to remind us all of daddy. Daddy had a dream, a dream to preach God's word and to lead many to Christ. His dream was to be an effective voice in the community, to take action when needed and to love people unconditionally with compassion and fearlessness. He had a dream to be a strong provider, a wonderful husband and awesome father and grandfather to us all, we, us, this family have a charge to continue the legacy of our fathers dream. As I continue in telling my story of the dream I had the night before, I notice that I have the attention of everyone in the room, all eyes on me and all ears listening to the sound of my voice, therefore I proceed…

"My dream takes me back to the day I reminisced on not too long ago, while sitting in my bay window watching the Saturday Morning Rain. I was thinking about one particular day when RJ and I were playing in the rain. Mama let us put on our yellow rubber boots and run up and down the driveway splashing in and out of puddles of water. She was so careful to make sure we had fun but came inside before daddy got home. We were so innocent and somewhat oblivious to all the things that were happening around us. Mama made the house a home, with her beauty and sophistication, our home was elegant, we knew we were loved. Daddy, a prominent figure in the community, respected, loved and honored by so many, never once did I think he had flaws.

So many things changed from that innocent moment of adolescence. My parents changed, my brother changed, I changed. I look over at RJ and tell him how much I admired and adored him, he was the perfect big brother. He came to all my dance recitals and plays, he stood up for me when jealous bullies tried to come at me and he was a good keeper of secrets. Not once did he tell a soul that I lost my virginity at 18 by a boy named Raymond White. I was smitten with Ray, we dated for 2 years, he was handsome, funny and patient with me because I was determined to hold on to my virginity until marriage but after my freshman year of college, I gave him my virtue and he never came around again. I was so hurt and RJ was there to comfort me, he even wanted to beat Ray up but he could never find him. I guess that's why by the time I got to 2nd year college and fell in love with Jeff, I felt the need to commit myself to him in a way that I thought would make him stay. You were right Jeff, I say as I look over at him, you were right when you told Brittany that I trapped you into marrying me, I did. To tell the truth, although I did fall in love with you, I never really loved you the same way I loved Raymond, I was scared and wanted to do the right thing for the sake of my family and our reputation. For that I must say I'm sorry and ask for your forgiveness. If you want your freedom now, I will give it to you, I totally understand if you did. You don't have to address that now, that's a conversation that you and I need to have one on one at a later time. Jeff nods his head in agreement, looking shocked that Nadine is holding herself together so cool and calmly. "RJ" , she says looking at him and laughs, you are my ACE, I love you so much brother, I'm super proud of you and the man you have become.

I'm so sorry that you and dad weren't as close as you would have liked to be, all because of a stupid misunderstanding. Dad wanted you to go to college, a major university, play a sport and maybe even follow in his footsteps to preach but that was never your forte. You were always in the kitchen with mama and Roxi, you loved to cook and I remember, when we were kids, you would be in my little pink kitchen cooking the best invisible vittles more than I was. I'm so sorry that you were misunderstood, I hurt for you still to this day due to the argument you and daddy had over your sexuality. Dad accused you of being gay because you liked to cook and never had a lot of girlfriends. He didn't know your pain, he never knew that it hurt you that the girls didn't pay much attention to you because you were on the chunky side. As handsome and as sweet of a person you are, the girls wanted a rough neck, a bad boy and that wasn't you. You were always mannerable, so sweet and so kind.

I remember our conversations late at night, while mom and dad were sleeping, we'd be in the kitchen and you would whip up some waffles or chocolate chip cookies and we'd binge on sweets and talk about our love life or lack thereof. Remember when you told me that you ate through your depression, all throughout high school through college. I was so happy for you when you married your first wife Gloria right after you graduated from college. You finally found love and I knew she loved you because she hung in there with you when you were going from job to job, not being stable because you just weren't happy with sitting behind a desk. It broke your heart when you found out that she couldn't have children and she lied and said she was pregnant but lost the baby. All of us were devastated to find out that she was barren way before you got married and that she kept that secret from you knowing how much you wanted a child. You were never able to recover from that and my heart broke for you when you divorced and she moved back to Puerto Rico with her family.

A few years later, when you met Shannon, you were in culinary school, just about to graduate and I remember how excited you were to take her out. I was apprehensive about your relationship because everything moved so fast but I know you truly love her. Shannon, I'm so sorry for mistreating you because you are white, I didn't trust you at first but I know you love my brother and it was you that helped make his catering business the success it is today. I ask for your forgiveness, from the both of you because you experienced racism from us, we tried to hide our wicked thoughts but we know why you all stopped coming around so much, we know it was the snide comments about Shannon's cooking or being a gold digger made you pull away from us, even when you all were simply trying to share the love you had for one another with us. Shannon gets up and gives me a hug, with tears in her eyes, she accepts my apology and so does RJ. Before I knew it, the whole room was teary eyed but I had to keep going as the Holy Spirit was leading. I had to address my children before I addressed my mom. Brandon and Brittany, I love you both with all my heart, you are the joy that keeps me breathing, you are my reason for living. Even when I thought I wasn't gonna make it through my surgery and cancer ordeal, the thought of leaving you gave me the strength to hang on. Brandon, ever since you were a little boy, we've always been close. You have always been so protective of me. Remember when you were about 5 years old and we were in the grocery store and a man was flirting with me, you ran up to that stranger, kicked him in the leg and told him to leave your mama alone.

I knew then you would be my personal watch guard, you've always had my back, even the times when I frustrated you, complaining about your choice of girlfriends, you still stood by me and for that, you'll always have a special place in my heart. Now, Brittany, you and I have had our ups and downs. I never realized how much you were hurting, I never knew until recently that you were carrying so much anger towards me by what you were being told. I'm so sorry you felt like you couldn't trust me enough to come talk to me, I apologize for not being there for you like I should, all because I felt rejected by you but was too much of a coward to come and talk to you. I love you so much and only want what's best for you and I pray that this day will bring a new found relationship between us, I pray that you have a heart to receive me. Aunt Ruby, you know I love you, you've always been my favorite aunt and I appreciate how you loved my daddy, I honor you today.

Then, I get quiet, I look at my mama and simply tell her, "mama, you are the strongest, smartest, classiest most beautiful woman I know, I wish I had you strength and patience… but before I could finish, I just break down crying, I could no longer hold all of these emotions inside. The tears just seemed to flow freely and I could not control it. Before I knew it, everyone in the room was crying so hard, we all started hugging on each other, people started apologizing to one another, there was talk all through the room, even my niece Jessica came to me and told me she loved me and apologized for stealing some perfume out of my room. I never knew she did that, I thought I had left it somewhere or lost it. Jeff and I embrace, he apologized to me for all the emotional turmoil he caused, he said he was sorry for not being an attentive husband and he regretted keeping the secret about Carla. Speaking of Carla, I looked across the room and noticed that she was just sitting there, watching all of us weep and hug each other, she looked so uncomfortable.

I questioned if I should go and hug her or say something but thought that would be too awkward so I get everyone's attention. "Okay everyone, enough of this cry fest, let's go ahead and take care of business because we don't want to keep Miss Carla waiting. She said, "oh no, it's no problem, I'm okay". She spoke so softly and put her head back down, I could tell she was super uncomfortable and felt out of place. So we all dry our tears and sit back down. Roxi brings in fresh lemonade and cookies, she must have been standing at the door listening this whole time because she was crying too. Jeff stands up and begins to officially read dad's will, he goes through all the formalities before he gets to the nitty gritty. It was ironic because my dad apologized to my mom in his letter, he made mention of his infidelity, Carla and her mom, that part nearly broke mama because although she knew what was mostly in his will, apparently she wasn't expecting that part but she did know that he left her the house, stocks, bonds and an undisclosed amount of money he has in an offshore bank account. He left all of his grandkids $50,000 each that they can get once they turn 18 and graduate from high school. My twins give each other a high five because they are old enough to receive their inheritance now. He left RJ his Bentley and gave him and Shannon $150, 000, there was also a sealed letter written to RJ that he was to read in private. I'll have to remind myself to ask him what it said later, then he left Roxi $30,000 and he left aunt Ruby their mama's wedding ring that he had for years that he never chose to give her even when she asked for it, he said whenever she marries Fred he would give it to her, plus he gave her $40,000. Surprisingly he left me and Jeff the deed to the church and $150,000 along with a letter on how he wanted us to keep his legacy alive at the church.

Jeff said the deed was something new and recent that he added right before he died. I was shocked, I thought for sure he would leave the church to mama and from the look in her eyes, she thought the same thing. Then finally, he said, if his plan to have Carla there worked out, he wanted her to be here to receive all the jewelry that her mama had given him over the years. Jeff pulls out a brown jewelry box that none of us had ever seen before and hands it over to Carla, she grabs it and puts it on her lap and looks back up at Jeff expecting him to say more, however he said that was the end of the reading of the will.

There were other matters of business that dad instructed Jeff to do with the board of directors of the church and a hedge fund he wanted distributed to his former business partners. So, that was it, dad's will was read and God's plan prevailed. There seemed to be a great sigh of relief coming from all of us. I think the tears of forgiveness released the pain that we all had been carrying for such a long time. I knew this wouldn't be the final conversations but it broke the ice and opened doors for more conversations of healing to come. Then mama taps dad's desk with a pen to get all of our attention one last time. She said, I have to make another announcement before you all leave.

So we all sat back down wondering what in the world could she have to say now. She proceeds to tell us that she has prayed about it and decided to take a sabbatical. She is going back to Virginia with cousin Mary for a few weeks because she needs to get away from this house and grieve privately. She said Roxi would be here to take care of everything and she hopes that we would allow her to do this to give her time to heal in her own way without worrying about her. We all looked shocked but for some reason, I'm not surprised, I can still feel the pain in mama's heart because of dad's cheating and Carla being the result of it.

I cannot imagine what she has or had to endure all these years. So we all humbly receive mom's decision and give her our blessing. Then mama turns to Carla and says, "my dear, I am so sorry that you never really got a chance to know your father. I do know that he loved you and I hope you understand why he couldn't bring you around the family, my heart goes out to you and I hope that you will take some time to get to know your brother and sister, hoping you all can get some sort of relationship in the future". Thank you for coming to my home, now if you all will excuse me... She leaves the room and RJ and I are looking at each other, I'm not sure how to respond so I go over to Carla and say, " if you ever need anything or just want to talk, I'm here. I reach out to hug her but she just gives me a little church pat and says okay. This was such an awkward moment, it seemed as though we needed to talk things through, there was so much more to be said but no one knew where to start. RJ walks up here and says, " well it's nice to meet you, I'm RJ and that's my family over there". He points to Shannon and the kids. He apologizes for his anger and just tells Carla he hopes that she understands how much of a shock this is to all of us. He then walks away, I can see the sweat beads on his baldhead. I had never seen my brother so nervous or anxious before. So I'm still standing there, it was an awkward moment because I didn't know what else to say or do. As I look across the room, I notice that my kids have left dad's study, heading somewhere with mama. Jeff is packing all the paperwork back into his briefcase and then there's an awkward silence again. Then I say, "do you want anything to drink or food to take with you?' She said no and grabbed her purse and said to me, it was so nice to finally meet all of you, this is a beautiful home, it must have been so nice to grow up here, sounding sarcastic. I nod and say yes it was, it wasn't perfect but it's home and you're welcome to visit us anytime, I'd like to get to know you better. I ask for her phone number and I give her mines knowing we'd probably never call each other.

I could tell by the way she gave me her number that she really wasn't interested. Then, Jeff comes along saying, "Carla are you ready to go back to your hotel, she says yes and he gives her the keys to his car, then her phone rings and she excused herself. So I look at Jeff and say, I guess we have a lot to talk about? Yea, he says, we do but not today, I think we all need a breather and take all of this in for a moment. We'll have breakfast tomorrow and then you and I can talk okay? He leans in and gives me a kiss on the cheek. I don't know what that means but I guess I'll find out tomorrow. I'm not sure if he still wants our marriage to work or not, heck I'm not even sure at this point. So much has happened and even though we all forgave one another, there's still the process of healing that needs to take place. I'm just glad that I obeyed God, I let the Holy Spirit do the talking and He broke the chains. So Jeff walks out headed to use the bathroom before hopping in his car to take Carla back to her hotel, I catch Aunt Ruby in the dining room packing a huge doggy bag, she seems very happy to have received a blessing from her brother. She said, chile I'm gonna take some of this food to Fred, I know he's hungry and probably still in that car knocked out. She said, " let me know when Diane is planning to leave, I wanna see her before that so I can say goodbye.

I tried to tell her just now but she's locked up in that room with Roxi again, boy I tell you, you would think that Roxi was her mama or something. Nah, they're just super close, remember Roxi helped raise mama when she was younger. I could hear the twins in the kitchen talking, sound like they were still eating and packing food to go. Mama had so much food in this house, I'm sure she didn't care if we took it all, she wasn't eating anyway. So I tell everyone goodbye, I go find cousin Mary and tell her to make sure she takes good care of my mama and that I would be back over here before they left. Now, you know she's in good hands with me, I'm gonna make sure she rests and eats, she'll be fine, she said as she gives me the sweetest hug, I love cousin Mary so much, I'm thankful that mama is going with her, she doesn't't' need to be alone right now, especially not in this house and even thought Roxi is here, I think some time away from here would do mama so good. I went back to dad's study to grab my purse and noticed that Carla left her inheritance, she actually left this jewelry box on the seat of her chair, so I hurry and grab it and run to take it to her before she and Jeff leave. I really wanted to open it to see what was in the box but I didn't. I ran outside but didn't see her in Jeff's car so I asked Fred, who had been laying down in his car this whole time, whether he saw the short lady who came with Jeff. He said, "yeah, she went around the side of the house towards the rose garden. So I walked towards the garden and I could hear Carla talking on the phone, she sounded pissed, so I hid alongside the big bush and listened to her conversation. I could not believe what I was hearing. Carla was on the phone fussing, saying, " can you believe this, this nigga just left me some junk jewelry that my mama bought for him, he didn't leave me no damn money at all, Todd, I didn't come all the way here just to leave with nothing, I want my money, they are gonna pay for this uncle Todd.

I'm thinking to myself, Todd? She said that twice, now I know it can't be my Todd, well, he's not my Todd but my former nurse and friend Todd, no way, he wouldn't know her, she's from New Orleans and Todd lives here. So I keep listening to the conversation but my heart is racing, then I hear her say, I paid you good money and pulled a lot of strings for you to end up being her nurse and you didn't even do what you were supposed to do and now I'm supposed to leave here with nothing? Oh hell no, this ain't over. Meet me at my hotel in about 30 minutes, we've got to come up with another plan. I'm not leaving Cedar City until I have my vengeance and my money". She hangs up the phone and I turn and quickly run back to the car to pretend to talk to Fred as he was still waiting on aunt Ruby.

He asked me if I found the girl I was looking for and I said yea but she's on the phone so I stand there to make more small talk with him then Aunt Ruby walks out the door with bags of food telling everyone bye, as she walks to the car, Carla walks from around the corner with a phony smile on her face, she's walking towards the door probably realizing she left her jewelry box so I yell towards her, "you forgot your jewelry box" as I hold it up so she can see it. Oh, thanks she said, I was wondering what I did with it. She walks towards Fred's car trying to put on a calm face, not realizing I heard every word. I'm trying my best to keep my composure and not slap the hell out of her when she gets in reaching distance. I hand her the box and wish her well. All the time I want to crack her in her face and I'm feeling sick to know that Todd, my nurse, the one who almost wooed me into falling in love with him has been in on this scam this whole time. I cannot believe this. I don't know what to do, who can I tell?

I need to get to RJ but do I really want to add more fuel to his flame? I can't tell mama, she's hurting enough, I don't want to tell the kids, they've been through enough already and I cannot tell Jeff, heck I don't trust him either, as far as I know, he's in on this whole plan. What exactly was the plan? Were they trying to extort money from my father, from my family? To blackmail us or what. My dad was a financial counselor and investor for over 40 years, he built his business from the ground up. He made a lot of people rich and got rich doing it. Many people thought that he was one of those fake prosperity preachers but he wasn't . He put his heart and soul into that church and didn't need to take up an offering to build it so for Carla, her mama and even her damn uncle Todd to think that they're gonna come up in here and take what's rightfully ours, what belongs to me, they got another thought coming. I go back in the house and grab my purse, I didn't even say bye to no one, I get in my car and drive, I'm not conscious of where I'm going, I'm just driving. I'm mad as hell and gotta figure out what I'm going to do about this Miss Carla and her schemes to try to come in here and wreak havoc over my family.

Oh! She just doesn't know who I am, she messing with the wrong somebody. I'm driving like a bat out of hell, somehow I end up in the parking lot of the Hyatt Regency in downtown. Is this where this chic is staying? I don't even remember how I know that, Jeff must have mentioned it in passing. All I know is that I'm here and I'm gonna wait near this front door. I wanna see Jeff drop her off, I want to know if he is going to go up and meet her and Todd, I want to truly know if it is Todd Ellis and not some other man. So I sit and wait, I wait 40 minutes and then I see Jeff's car pull up at the front door. Carla exists with a purse and a jewelry box in hand, she gets out and looks pissed, she probably cussed Jeff out all the way here because she didn't get any money. As soon as she slams his door, he pulls off. I watch to see if he's gonna park or exit.

He leaves, whew! He didn't stay, that still doesn't mean much but at least he's not here right now. So I wait a little longer to see if Todd shows up. Fifteen minutes later, I see this tall, dark handsome man with his signature shades on walking from the parking lot to the front door. I didn't see him pull in so I can recognize the car but as he walks close to the door, its him, doggone it, it is Todd. What the hell? I'm livid!!! So this was all a plan, somehow, she arranged for him to be my nurse, what was he supposed to do seduce me, influence me to have sex with him? What was the plan, to get me in a compromising position and take pics of me? This is some lifetime movie channel stuff. Wow! I cannot believe it, I just can't believe it. All this to hurt my family and take my daddy's money, to humiliate me and my family! I cannot believe this!

My heart is beating so fast it's hurting, I need to get out of here before I have a heart attack. The tears begin to roll down my face, my stomach is in knots, this is unreal. I've been bamboozled! I nearly lost my family for this man. My dad is gone, my mom is leaving, don't know if my husband is gonna leave me. I can't do this, I can't handle all of this. I don't know what to do next. I need to get to RJ but I need to get home first but I can't drive, my hands and legs are shaking like leaves. Just when I thought the fire was being put out, Carla came and poured fuel back on the flames, just like I thought, this was too good to be true, I felt something in the pit of my stomach, my discernment is strong yet I couldn't' put my finger on this storm brewing but now I know what it is, it's called Carla's Revenge.

www.ingramcontent.com/pod-product-compliance
Lightning Source LLC
LaVergne TN
LVHW020647100826
845148LV00012B/2360